THE PONY CLUE

MARY GERVAISE

Armada

CONTENTS

CHAPTER ONE

TOLD IN CONFIDENCE

THE new girl's name was Petronella, which seemed rather weighty for a pocket-sized person whose uniform was so much too big. She was home-sick already, though the spring term was barely two hours old.

"I suppose," she murmured to Georgia Kane, who had been asked to look after her until Miss Giles, the kindergarten mistress, arrived, "I suppose *you've* been here for years!"

Georgie smiled at the drooping nine-year-old.

"Not quite," she answered cheerfully. "The Grange wasn't turned into a school till last year. It opened in January—about a year ago to the day." She added with pride, "I was one of the first lot, of course."

"And—is it nice?" faltered Petronella.

Nice! What a word, Georgie thought, to use for the Grange, High Lennet, Dorset, which was such a beautiful, gracious old house, as well as the best school in England!

"Yes, it's very nice," she said reassuringly, "and you'll soon get to like it. I say, this wind's rather fierce, isn't it? Let's go and have a look at the stables now."

Petronella nodded, and they hurried across the garden to the stable yard. The new-comer had already announced that she had ridden since she was three, though never on hard roads. She was an Australian, in England for the first time.

At the sight of the stables her whole manner changed.

"Why," she breathed delightedly, "I never thought it would be like this!! The pictures I saw were pretty good, but they didn't give you any idea. Which pony can I have? Do we ride bareback? Do we play polo? What's *this* one's name, and *this?"*

Georgie gave a sigh of relief. Petronella was all right now! When a chauffeur had solemnly delivered her at the door, like a parcel, just as Georgie and her friends Susan and Ermyn had arrived, she had looked so white and ill that everyone had felt worried. That was why Miss Primrose, the head mistress, had asked Georgie to take charge of Petronella at once and show her round the grounds.

It had been disappointing to have to go off like that, without greeting the rest of the Fourth, or even seeing in which room one was to sleep. It was trying, too, to have to amuse this forlorn little new girl who was so grimly determined not to show how miserable she felt. But now the ice was broken, and the ponies, thought Georgie, could do the rest.

"I like this chestnut!" cried Petronella. "And the skewbald. He looks like a clown."

"Well, the girls he belongs to call him Pierrot," laughed Georgie, but her hazel eyes were resting, in proud affection, on the beautiful chestnut pony who had turned to look at Petronella. She said, reaching out to pat his glossy neck, "This one's mine. His name is Spot. And I know he hasn't any spots! He was given that name before I had him."

"He's lovely!" Petronella, who was very small for her age, had to stand on tiptoe to stroke him. "I had a pony called Turkey, and you'll never guess why. Give it up? Well, you know the Turkish flag? He had a moon and a star on his forehead, just like that. He had to be shot when Daddy died. . . . And once he was nearly stolen. There aren't any horse thieves in England, are there?"

Georgie hesitated, unwilling to tell this excitable child that there had been, in fact, an attempt to steal Miss Primrose's own beautiful thoroughbred, Mademoiselle. Petronella did not notice her silence.

"Turkey was lovely," she said wistfully. "But these are lovely too."

The stables at The Grange consisted of three blocks of buildings, and Georgie took Petronella to the part where the smaller ponies were kept. She patted them, and was soon calling Pixie and Pumpkin, Jumbo, Squib, and the rest by their names.

"And there's the little donkey!" she exclaimed, spying a small brown figure who was watching Georgie from her loose box. "I know *her* name—she's Penelope! There was a special picture of her!"

Georgie was rather puzzled. She stroked the little donkey's face—Penelope was her property really, though considered the mascot of the whole school—and looked at Petronella.

"Which pictures do you mean?" she asked.

"They were in a newspaper," the child said vaguely. "There was a whole page about the Grange, and lots of photos. We don't get many papers on our station, so everyone had a look, and

Auntie said that was the school for me. I wanted to keep the pictures, but our head stockman borrowed the paper and lost it. And then Auntie cabled some friends and asked them to meet me at London docks, and they said they would. So I came over in a ship, and they did meet me, and here I am. But I guess I'd sooner be back in Australia, even though Mummy and Daddy—aren't there any more . . ."

Scowling fiercely, Petronella dared Georgie to be sorry for her. Georgie took the hint and answered in a matter-of-fact tone.

"I didn't want to come to school a bit, but I'm glad I did. You'll feel the same. I don't know a single girl who doesn't like it here. Listen—I hear some of them coming now. Good, they're juniors, so I'll be able to introduce you."

Petronella gasped and seemed to grow smaller than ever. A bevy of First and Second formers came into the stable with old Maxwell, the head groom. When they spotted Georgie, the juniors rushed forward, because in her first term at the Grange, when she couldn't ride, she had often helped the kindergarten mistress.

"Georgie!" squeaked little Nancy Andrews, capering up to her. "I'm going to start jumping this term!"

She had been very delicate when Georgie first knew her, but now she looked quite different and glowing with health. Georgie looked at her watch as if she were in a hurry, and asked Nancy to show Petronella Smith the rest of the stables. Then, exchanging grins with Maxwell, she made her escape and ran back to the school building to find her friends.

They were all there—red-haired Susan, and

Ermyn, Dandy, and Pam, and Anne Conway, who had just been moved up into the Fourth.

"We've been wondering where on earth you'd got to," Susan said, grabbing Georgie's arm. "We're not sleeping in Bedroom Eight any more—we've been put in Thirteen! It's the biggest room of them all—it holds nine. Look!"

She showed Georgie the typed list which had been pinned up on the big baize-covered notice board hanging in the entrance hall. "BEDROOM XIII," it was headed:

Anne Conway	Judy Thurston
Dandy Jones	Susan Walker
Georgia Kane	Catherine Wilkinson
Ermyn Mauleverer	Constance Wilkinson
Pamela Pinkerton	

The last two names were new to Georgie, and she gave a little gasp.

"Don't say we've got twins again, the very term after the Daneforths have left!" she exclaimed.

Pat and Peach Daneforth had been great friends of hers, and everyone at the Grange was sorry that this attractive and gifted pair had left. But their parents believed in travel, and they were now at school in Switzerland. Fortunately they lived only a few miles from Georgie's Devonshire home, so she would always meet them in the holidays.

"Yes, the Wilkinsons are twins all right," said Susan, "though you'd never guess it by looking at them. Constance isn't bad, but Catherine! They're with Matron now, and that reminds me: Miss Primrose wants you to go to her study."

"Now, why on earth——?" wondered Ermyn.

"I thought we were all to do our unpacking before tea. Why, Georgie hasn't had *time* to do anything wrong yet!"

"Perhaps you're being pushed up into the Fifth, Georgie," suggested Judy Thurston, who was one of the best horsewomen in the school. She and her two elder sisters all bore a strong resemblance to the horses they loved so well, but when they were not actually in the saddle they were quiet, rather colourless people who liked to get into a rut and stay there.

"No," said Pam Pinkerton, of the dancing eyes and short black hair, "there are no removes this term, except in Anne's case. I'm glad we're still Fourth, though the form will have to be divided into A and B now it's got so big."

"It'll be super in Thirteen," gloated Ermyn; "now we'll be able to do all the things they do in the school stories I've read—midnight feasts, and pillow fights——"

Howls of derision from the rest drowned her words.

"Kids' stuff!" cried Dandy. "And you *know* how tiny the bedrooms are. Thirteen's the only big one there is, and even so the nine beds will be simply squashed in. That's the worst of the Grange getting so popular."

"Ah!" said Susan, with a maddening superiority. "You ought to have been here at the beginning. *Then* we were really select!"

She was only teasing, of course, but Dandy coloured angrily. Her sense of humour was not a very strong one, and she was always conscious that she was not one of the pioneers of the Grange, but had arrived for its second term.

"Select or not, we haven't had the sort of picnic we'll have *this* term," she retorted, "all herded into Thirteen. It won't be the same place at all!"

"Why are you all down here?" asked a new voice—a quiet but decisive voice, belonging to Ruth Conway, the head girl. She stood on the stairs, straight and tall, and looked at the group of Fourth formers. "Go up to your dormitories, please," she said; "and is Georgia here? Oh, there you are. Didn't you get the message from Miss Primrose?"

"Oh, I'm sorry!" Georgie jumped guiltily and made for the head mistress's study. She felt a little ruffled. She had hardly seen the others yet, or compared notes about the holidays . . .

"Come in. Well, Georgia, I'm sorry to call you away from your friends," said Miss Primrose, just as if she had read Georgie's rebellious thoughts, "and I'm very grateful to you for having looked after Petronella Smith. It's hard to be on one's own at nine years old. She is an orphan, you see, and the elderly couple who have adopted her live in a very remote part of Australia, which is why they have sent her here to be educated. Sit down, my dear. I hope you had a lovely Christmas?"

"Oh, yes, thank you, Miss Primrose. Susan and Ermyn were staying with us, and we did have fun." Georgie, smiling at the head mistress, did not tell her how Susan's mare, Black Agnes, had died during that holiday, which was why Plum Pudding, the new pony, had made his appearance at the Grange. Miss Primrose, who took such an interest in them all, must surely know that already.

"I understand that your riding's coming on.

There will be the usual gymkhana in Randall's Meadow, towards the end of the term, and I hope you will enter for some of the events. But I shall give out the details later. Georgia——"

Miss Primrose hesitated, and if she had been anyone else Georgia would have thought she was nervous. The head mistress of the Grange was young, slender yet strong, with dark hair and steady blue eyes. She was brilliant and imaginative, and a splendid horsewoman who, though fearless herself, understood very well the problems which people less experienced had to face. All the girls liked and respected her, and the school which she had started as an experiment was becoming more and more of a success. But Georgie, who had begun her life there handicapped by a real terror of horses, felt a deep gratitude as well.

She waited now, wondering what Miss Primrose was going to say. The familiar oak-panelled study looked just as usual, with its cheerful fire and the lazy black cat purring in front of it, but somehow there was something disturbing in the atmosphere. Miss Primrose was a little paler than she remembered, and perhaps her smile was less serene.

"Do you read school stories, Georgia?" was the totally unexpected question.

"Why—yes, Miss Primrose. Some. But—as someone was saying just now—one gets a bit tired of the usual things, like midnight feasts and pillow fights, and schools being burnt down . . ."

Miss Primrose laughed. "The stock situations! And yet, you know, *we* nearly had a fire last year, didn't we? And I seem to remember an unorthodox picnic last summer. But what I'm leading up to is this. I think you must have read stories in which the head mistress's niece arrives at the school?"

"Oh, yes," said Georgie, "I've read several. And she's usually perfectly awful till the last

"Do you read school stories, Georgia?"

chapter . . . Oh!! Have *you* got a niece, Miss Primrose?"

"Not quite, but it seems that I have a young cousin, of whose existence I knew nothing until a fortnight ago. Georgia—you realize that what I'm telling you is in confidence. Mine is a rather complicated family. You have met my nephew, and I remember your surprise upon realizing that he is actually older than myself. I told you then that my father had married twice, and that my nephew is the son of my half-brother. He is also—or so I thought until recently—the only member left of the Primrose family. I knew that one of my father's cousins had settled in Australia——"

"Petronella!" gasped Georgie before she could stop herself.

"No. Petronella is merely a coincidence. My cousin, who is coming to the Grange this term, is called Valerie, and she's older than you—she's sixteen—so she'll probably be in the Fifth. But she's very shy—much more so than you ever were—and I thought I would tell you all this so that you could make her feel at home. You seem to be good at that. She'll soon settle down, I'm sure, but it *will* be difficult, especially as I don't want to show her any special consideration. You see, I have read some of those stories myself," said Miss Primrose, a twinkle in her eye, "and for Valerie's sake, and my own, there must be no idea of favouritism."

"I'll do my best, of course," said Georgie, "but if she's sixteen, she won't want *me* very much, will she? But I do think it's exciting! Did she just come in one day and say, 'I'm your long-lost cousin'?"

"No, because she wasn't lost at all—it's simply that she, or rather her mother, has just found me! Her father was my real cousin, you see, but he died several years ago, and Valerie and her mother lived in Sydney. Then her mother married again, and they came to England and naturally decided to see if there were any Primroses left in Lennet. And when they discovered that the old family house was a school, they arranged that Valerie should come to it."

"Does she want to?" Georgie asked bluntly, aware of a certain uneasiness in the mistress's manner.

"No, I'm afraid she doesn't. I've met her only once, when her mother brought her down here last week. But she's shy, as I told you, and she's not fond of riding, and I'm afraid there may be many difficulties ahead of her. She'll be arriving tomorrow. Well, that's all, I think. Perhaps there won't be an opportunity for you to do anything."

"If I can, I will," Georgie promised; thinking of all the people who could have looked after Valerie far better. She did not enumerate them, however, because Miss Primrose must know her own business best. Still, it was queer, and a little annoying, to be asked to look after someone like this.

"Do you mind very much, Georgia?"

"Oh, no, Miss Primrose, not a bit. At least, not *very* much," answered Georgie, who was truthful by nature. "Only, won't she think it cheek? When I'm only Fourth, I mean . . ."

"No. She hasn't been to school before, and distinctions of that kind won't mean much to her. You still look puzzled, Georgia."

"I was just wondering," Georgie admitted, "why you said this talk was in confidence. If everyone knows that Valerie's a relation . . ."

"I want you to be friendly of your own accord," said Miss Primrose, "not to broadcast the fact that you have been asked to look after her. She is—unusual and, having found your own feet so well, I am hoping that you can help her to find hers. Now, that's enough about Valerie. I'm afraid I have made you very late for tea, but it's being served in detachments today, as there are still several people to come. Off you go!"

Georgie walked pensively to the dining-room. She was not looking forward to the job she had undertaken. It seemed too silly for words to have to act as nannie to a girl two years older than herself, yet common sense told her that Miss Primrose would not have made her request unless she had thought it necessary.

The faithful Susan was waiting for her in the refectory, which was practically empty. The maids were clearing the tables, murmuring in low tones. One was sweeping up the remains of a cup and saucer and a piece of crumby cake.

"What's happened?" asked Georgie, sinking into a chair.

"Catherine Wilkinson's been in here, throwing a temperament!" Susan said dramatically. "Talk about new girls! They're more bother than they're worth."

Georgie, busy with a ham sandwich, nodded in heartfelt agreement. As Dandy Jones had remarked earlier, the Grange was not the same place at all!

CHAPTER TWO

STORM CLOUDS!

LEAVING Miss Primrose's study, Georgie had wondered what she would say if people asked her what the interview had been about. She soon saw, however, that there was no need to worry on that account. The Middle School was buzzing with one topic only—the truly appalling behaviour of Catherine Wilkinson!

"You'll see for yourself in a moment, when we're unpacking," Susan said, as she absent-mindedly worked through a second tea to keep Georgie company. "Lots of people are queer—look how weird Ermyn was when she first came, with all that 'Child of the Circus' business. But she *was* civilized, and Catherine isn't. Why, she brought a pad and pencil in to tea with her, and there she sat, pushing her food away because she said she wasn't hungry, sketching people right and left. So Matron confiscated her pencil, and then Catherine absolutely lost her rag and jumped up and hurled the cup and saucer on the ground. And Rosalie, who knows her at home, says she's always like that."

"That's beside the point," Georgie said quickly, remembering how in the past Rosalie Hall, also of the Fourth, had had her knife into *her*. "It isn't fair to rake up what people do at home. But Catherine certainly does sound the last word in new girls! What's the other twin like?"

"Oh, quite calm," replied Susan; "short, plump, and placid, while Catherine's tall, thin, and wild. She's deaf, by the way—Constance is, I mean. She had an illness and it left her deaf, but she's getting better, so we're not to worry, Matron says. Just be ordinary. She can lip-read and all that. My hat, she must be *glad* to be deaf if Catherine makes the same row at home as she makes here!"

"Can they ride?" asked Georgie—that being the question which one automatically asked at the Grange.

"Yes. They share a pony—Starbright. They've

brought her with them—we saw the van drive up when you were with Miss Primrose. She's a thoroughbred, Rosalie says . . ."

"Would you like another sandwich, Miss Georgie?" inquired a smiling maid. "And how about you, Miss Susan? I'll cut them in a minute——"

"No, thank you, Maureen," said Georgie, jumping up and flashing Susan a warning look. "We've kept you too late as it is, but it was a lovely tea. Come along, Sue!"

They flew up to Bedroom Thirteen, which was in the usual state of first-night chaos. It had been one of the attics originally, which was why it was so large. It had a sloping ceiling, and at first glance the windows seemed too small, but they had been made to open wide, and so there was plenty of air. Bedroom Twelve, where the rest of the Fourth-formers slept, was also on the top floor. The views from these upper rooms were simply wonderful.

"Call this a school! *What* a dump!" a clear voice was saying when Georgie and Susan reached the door of Thirteen. And that was their introduction to Catherine Wilkinson.

New as she was, she had already managed to rumple her green uniform skirt in a most surprising way. Tall and lanky, she lounged in her cubicle, lower lip thrust out, and straight dark hair tumbling into her eyes.

"Hallo!" said Georgie, trying to do her duty. "You're Catherine, aren't you? I hope you're going to like it here."

"Why?" snapped Catherine.

"What?" asked Georgie, startled, and everybody laughed. Everybody, that is, except a quiet-looking girl in the next cubicle, who was sorting her clothes into neat piles on the bed. She just looked round with a vague smile, and Georgie knew that this must be Constance.

"Why should you hope I like it here?" Catherine asked fiercely. "What's it to do with you?"

She had a clever, unusual face, with dark eyes under very heavy black brows. At the moment her lips were curled contemptuously.

"Well," Georgie said pleasantly, "I should think it's much nicer for other people if you *do* like a thing than if you don't. Is this your sister?"

"Yes, but she can't hear, so it's no use——" Catherine paused, frowning, as Georgie went up to the quiet girl and said, "Hallo, Constance!" in her usual tone of voice.

"Hallo!" the placid twin said at once.

"I say, Georgie," said Pam Pinkerton, who had been made the provisional Captain of the Fourth, "you'd better tell her who we all are."

"I shouldn't bother," said Catherine haughtily. "We shan't be staying. We've been expelled from three schools already, and we certainly shan't stay in a stuffy old-fashioned hole like this."

"Stuffy!" Susan swallowed her rage. "Why, the bathrooms and the stables are as modern as modern can be, and we *like* the oldness of everything else. Were you expelled for being rude?"

But before Catherine could rush into angry speech Georgie had taken down the list that was fastened with drawing-pins to the door, and was showing it to Constance, pointing out each girl in turn. She had never seen twins, or even ordinary sisters, less alike. Constance had a round, dimpled face with blue eyes and nice smooth brown plaits.

"Why does *she* have to be expelled every time Catherine is?" Ermyn demanded audibly, and to her dismay Constance read her lips.

"We haven't been expelled," she said in a very little voice; "only asked to leave. Catherine, you shouldn't say——"

"Shut up!" said her twin, with such ferocity that Constance obeyed on the spot.

"Well, let's put our things away," Pam said in relief, "Matron will be here any moment now. Georgie, you lucky thing, you've got the end cube and the best view. Which prefect's in charge of this dorm? Does it say on the list?"

"June is, for one," volunteered Judy Thurston, mentioning her eldest sister. The three Thurstons thought a great deal of one another.

"And Greta Davis is the second," said Georgie, fastening the list on the door again. Hearing an exclamation, she turned round and saw Catherine Wilkinson busy with pencil and paper, and Judy's face scarlet with anger.

In that split second the new girl had drawn a caricature of the eldest Thurston that was so clever, as well as so cruel, that nobody spoke for a little while. Then Matron came bustling in to see if the unpacking had been properly done, and the girls scattered guiltily to their cubicles. Catherine tossed the drawing on to her bed, not bothering at all to hide it.

Matron picked it up. Then she tore it across and gave its creator a long look.

"I see I shall have quite a collection of your pencils, Catherine, if you keep on drawing like this," she said evenly. "It isn't funny——"

"It isn't meant to be!" Catherine flung at her angrily. "We didn't want to come here—we——"

"Will you kindly put your clothes away? I haven't very much time," said Matron. "Best coats in that cupboard, everyone, in the corner—heavy coats will be kept in the cloak-room downstairs. What a nice photograph of your mother, Georgia—and, Anne, this a very good one of you and Ruth!"

"Yes, Uncle Gordon has a friend who's wizard at photography," said Anne. "I wish he'd come and take one of the whole school! Uncle Gordon did bring him down here last summer hols., and he got some smashing shots of the horses and the house, but of course we were all away."

"Let's see!" Catherine pushed Susan and Ermyn aside and marched into Anne's cubicle. "H'm, yes. Not bad," she said, surveying the photograph in question. As quick as lightning, she whipped out her pencil and pad again and copied the faces of the two Conway sisters, and held out the result for all to see. This time no one could object to what she had done. The likeness was extraordinary.

"Just a few lines and squiggles, and they *are* Ruth and Anne!" cried Georgie, and Ermyn squeaked, "Do *me!*"

Catherine gave her a slow, insolent smile.

"Sorry. I haven't time," she said.

Pretty little Ermyn, so dainty and doll-like for her fourteen years, was definitely not a person to be snubbed. Of all the girls at the Grange she was the most used to holding her own, for she had ridden in her father's circus since a very early age, and her wits were as keen as her muscles were strong.

Everyone waited for her to turn on the rash new girl, for Ermyn didn't put up with much as a rule. But she said nothing.

"I'll show you the kindergarten when you're

"It's not nearly *far enough away"*

ready, Catherine," said Susan sweetly. "They're very fond of drawing there too."

"Ha, ha," said Catherine, her dark eyes beginning to glitter angrily. "Let me tell you that an artist, a *real* artist, told me I oughtn't to be at school at all—I ought to be in Paris, studying . . ."

"Don't go to Pawwis," pleaded Ermyn, reviving the babyish lisp which had so annoyed everybody when she was new. *"Please* don't go to Pawwis, Catherine——"

"Why not?" the new girl asked in surprise.

"Because," Ermyn told her, "it's not *nearly* far enough away . . ."

Everyone burst out laughing. Catherine went back to her cubicle and pulled out the drawer at the bottom of her locker with such violence that she nipped the first two fingers of her right hand.

She gave a short cry, for the pain was intense. Matron gave up all idea of superintending the unpacking and led the white-faced girl to her sitting-room, where the medicine cupboard was kept.

"Serves her right," muttered Ermyn, and Dandy Jones, who was cowboy-minded, said, "I'm with you there, old-timer!"

"Well," said Georgie, with a shrug, "she did ask for it, didn't she? But——" Looking up, she encountered a puzzled, half-frightened glance from the other twin. Clearly Constance had been unaware of the incident and was now wondering where Catherine was.

"Tell her, Pam!"

"No, I can't. You tell her, Georgie."

So Georgie did—thinking, quite understandably, *"Oh, these new girls!"*

"Her hand isn't badly hurt, is it? Will it stop her drawing?" Constance asked in that very quiet voice of hers.

"No, I don't think so. I expect she'll be at supper," Georgie assured her, and then they all made a drive and tidied their cubicles as a surprise for Matron later on.

Catherine *was* at supper, but her presence cast a gloom over the whole refectory. Her right hand was bandaged, and Constance had to cut up her meat for her. Georgie and Susan, who sat at the same table as the Wilkinsons, knew by the sufferer's manner that she blamed Bedroom Thirteen for her misfortune, and not her own bad temper.

Rosalie Hall kept on glancing at her, and after supper she fastened on to Georgie.

"I say! How are you all settling down in Thirteen?" she wanted to know. "We're going to be quite cosy in Twelve. I'm thankful *we* haven't got that ghastly Catherine Wilkinson! Oh, Georgie, you know more about Miss Primrose's family than anyone: who's Valerie?"

"Valerie?" Georgie repeated, playing for time.

"Yes, it's on the door of Bedroom Nine, that little single one that Teepoo used to have. 'Valerie Primrose.' I asked Matron, and she said, 'A second cousin, who is coming tomorrow as a pupil in the school'." Rosalie, who really was a dreadful gossip, kept watching Georgie as she spoke.

"Oh well, then, Matron's *told* you who Valerie is," Georgie said lightly and slipped away.

It was a cold evening, being only January still, and so there were games in the big hall until bedtime. This was a good way of keeping warm and also of meeting old friends whom one had not been able to seek out till now.

Greta Davis, who played the piano beautifully, provided music for such games as required it, and soon embarked on some waltzes which set everybody's feet twinkling. Once, in a Paul Jones, Georgie found herself dancing with Barbara Snow, another Fourth-former and one of those jealous, dog-in-the-mangerish people who are always rather difficult, even when they try to be nice.

Barbara was trying now. She had been very hostile to Georgie when they were both new, and although they had buried the hatchet some time ago she was still envious of the girl she had once despised.

"Hallo, Georgie! Glad to be back? But I suppose you've had marvellous hols, as usual . . . I? Oh, I didn't do much. I don't like the idea of sleeping in attics, do you? Still, I'm glad I'm in Twelve and not Thirteen—Rosalie says that Catherine person is the limit. Have you got to look after her? You're usually told off to be kind to the new little lambs . . ."

"No," said Georgie thankfully, "I haven't got to look after her! She'll certainly provide some excitement."

"Talking of that," said Barbara, "did you read in the daily papers that some ancient caves have been unearthed just the other side of Randall's Meadow? That's more exciting than new girls hurling teapots all over the place. Rosalie says——"

The music changed and they had to march again. Rosalie seemed to be saying far too much, Georgie thought, feeling suddenly sorry for Catherine. But she dismissed the queer new girl from her mind as she wangled the next dance with Susan and told her about the caves.

"I know! Dandy told me just now. It was in the papers last week, but I don't know how it is—when I'm staying at your house, we're always too busy to read the news! They were scooped out of the hillside hundreds of years ago—or do I mean thousands? Anyway, I'm longing to see them. Of course," Susan ended blithely, "you know they're out of bounds . . ."

CHAPTER THREE

ENTER A STRANGER

"HOW good we are!" Susan remarked, snuggling down in her warm bed. "This is the first time there have ever been nine of us in one bedroom, and yet we haven't nattered half as much as we usually do, after lights-out on the first night of term."

"I don't feel good," said Ermyn. "Just sleepy, I guess."

"It doesn't seem like the first night, does it?" yawned Anne. "Such a lot has happened."

"If you mean *me*——!" Catherine Wilkinson began at once, but several people made haste to scotch that idea.

"You aren't as jolly important as all that, let me tell you!" came from Judy Thurston, who was still smarting at the thought of that cruel caricature of June. "We meant the school getting so much bigger—and coming up to this floor to sleep—and Susan Walker's new pony—and Miss Primrose's niece or cousin or whatever she is, coming here as a new girl——"

"I'm longing to see her," Pam declared. "You know, I feel sorry for her in a way. Miss Primrose is so fair that she'll probably be extra hard on her, to make sure she isn't favouring her at all. Valerie! Valeries are pretty as a rule—dark, and lively and gay."

Several people disagreed with this, saying that they

had known fair Valeries who were dull and plain to the point of gloom. Georgie lay low. She had made her own picture of Valerie Primrose. Shy—not fond of riding—disliking the idea of school . . .

"Georgie's quiet!" said Dandy, in her toughest whisper. Because she was considered delicate, she made a point of being rugged. "Cat got your tongue, Georgie?"

"I'm thinking about those caves," Georgie said quickly, and with truth. They *had* been at the back of her mind ever since she had heard of them. "I know Lennet is a very old village, but a discovery like this will put it on the map for a lot of people—my eldest brother, for instance."

"Oh, they're not as wonderful as all *that,*" put in Ermyn. "A sort of inner chamber has been discovered, but people have always known about the other part, and they used to be allowed to go inside till about twenty years ago. The caves were fastened up then, I believe, but now the rock's subsided, or something, and one can get in again. I'd like to have a dekko."

"They're out of bounds," Pam reminded her quickly.

"Does it matter so very much?" asked Ermyn wistfully.

"Of course it does. We're too old to break rules like that," was Pam's crisp reply. "We're trusted. I almost wish we weren't!"

Georgie knew just what she meant.

"If only Miss Primrose were a different sort of person," she said. "If she were a gorgon we *could* do these things. Still, we may see the caves on the gymkhana day. Good night, everybody."

Then she thought of something else.

"Catherine," she whispered, "does Constance know Morse?"

"A bit," was the grudging answer, "but you needn't trouble . . ."

However, Georgie leaned over Constance's bed and laboriously tapped out GOOD NIGHT on her pillow. If the deaf girl had been asleep this would not have disturbed her, but she was awake and said, "Good night, Georgia!" in a pleased tone. It was a moonlit night, and she had recognized the pyjama-clad figure.

"How like Georgie," Susan thought, "to remember that one can't lip-read in the dark!" and she picked up her torch and flashed the same message. This time Constance laughed outright and Greta, the prefect on duty that night, opened the door a few inches and said "Really!" in an exhausted voice which made them all feel very guilty indeed.

Next morning the various forms were re-assembled, books and stationery were given out, and new girls had a short test to do. Miss Primrose was unable to give her usual beginning-of-term talk, as she was very busy, but during a free period just before lunch Maxwell, the head groom, addressed the whole school in the big hall, explaining the stable rules and the standard of behaviour that was expected of the "G" girls when riding in public places. He was a dear old man and Georgie had a special affection for him, as he had done so much towards giving her confidence on horseback. All the same, she slipped away while he was still speaking, for—from the window by which she stood—she could see a tall, rather flashily-dressed figure ambling up the drive and guessed that it was Valerie.

"Good morning," Georgie said nervously. One couldn't say "Hallo!" to a girl who wore a short jacket of yellow fur over a tight black velvet skirt, and a green hat with a little veil perched on her much-waved hair.

"'Morning!" responded the stranger in a somewhat off-hand manner. "I've come to school here. I'm the Head's cousin. I suppose she's knocking about somewhere? I said I'd let her know when I was coming, but I thought it would be more bonzer to pop down on my own."

"I see," said Georgie faintly. *Bonzer?* She knew the Australian word, of course, but she hadn't heard it used quite like this before. Still, if it came to that, she had never before encountered a Valerie Primrose!

"Well," said the other breezily, "now that I *am* here, what about some tucker, eh?"

"And this," thought Georgie, "is the girl who's *shy!*" She tried to hide her dismay as she said quietly, "I saw you from the window and wondered if you'd lost your way. Please come in and I'll take you to Miss Primrose."

"What's the rush?" shrugged Valerie. "I told the taxi driver to drop me at the gate, because I wanted to look round actually. After all—old family abode and so forth. Rather dingy, though, isn't it?"

Georgie managed to control her wrath, but she did not trust herself to reply. *Dingy!*

"So weather-beaten," Valerie went on. "I wonder Cousin Bunty doesn't have it stuccoed."

"Cousin Bunty?" Georgie repeated in a feeble voice.

"Mum says the great head mistress used to call

herself Bunty when she was small, so that's what we call her now," Valerie said calmly. "Well, which is the way in? I could do with a gallon of tea!"

"We'll be having lunch soon," Georgie told her and added, as an attempt at conversation: "People drink lots of tea in Australia, don't they?"

Valerie smiled for the first time. She had rather more teeth than usual, Georgie thought, but it *was* a smile.

"I'll say we do. It's not the only thing I'm going to miss. Still, now I'm here, I'll give Cousin Bunty's school a chance . . ."

Georgie looked at the round pink face and wondered if its owner had any tact at all. Then she reminded herself that Miss Primrose had asked her especially to look after Valerie.

"We have another Australian girl," she said, leading the new-comer through the side door. Valerie minced along on high heels and carried a very elaborate plastic handbag. She looked much older than sixteen.

"What?" she said sharply. "Another Aussie? Here?"

"Yes," said Georgie, propelling her through the cloak-rooms. "She's only a junior—just nine, but I expect you'd like to talk to her."

Valerie snorted. "No fear! Kids bore me to sobs. Where does she come from, anyway? Not Sydney?"

"No. Victoria, I think—somewhere up country, anyway," Georgie said vaguely, feeling quite worn out with the effort of being pleasant to someone whose every word infuriated her afresh. "Here's Miss Primrose's study."

"Thanks," said Valerie. She did not even knock but flung the door open with a breezy cry of "Hallo, there! Here I am!"

Georgie felt a strong desire to giggle and rushed back to the hall. But Maxwell had finished his talk and the girls were going off to wash their hands ready for lunch.

"Hallo," Susan said to Georgie, "why on earth did you bolt like that? I saw you pass the window with a ghastly female in tow. Selling something, I s'pose. Did you get rid of her? I say, Maxwell thinks——"

"Sue," cut in Georgie. "That was Valerie! I mean, that *is* Valerie. She's come."

Susan clutched her head. "Excuse me while I swoon!" she cried, reeling backwards and treading violently on the toe of Miss Kennedy, who happened to be hurrying past.

When peace was restored the girls clustered round Georgie, longing to hear what Valerie was like; but Georgie was unwontedly reserved.

"You'll see for yourselves at lunch!" she said.

However, they didn't, because Valerie had hers in the study with Miss Primrose. Some of the girls—Barbara and Rosalie amongst the number—thought that this was favouritism, but Georgie knew that poor Miss Primrose was delaying the moment when Valerie would make her startling début.

"You might as least tell us what she looks like!" cried Pam.

"Oh, tall—with a marvellous tan, of course," Barbara cut in. "Australians always have that."

"Some haven't," said Ermyn. "Look at that little new kid Georgie got landed with yesterday—she's positively pasty!"

"Hush," said Georgie anxiously, "she'll hear." And, glancing at the juniors' tables, she saw that Petronella *had* heard, but—judging from her radiant smile—did not seem in the least offended by the reference to her complexion.

Seeing that no more was to be gleaned from Georgie as to the appearance of Valerie Primrose, the girls began to discuss other things.

"There's a mixed Senior and Middle School ride this afternoon. We've both been picked! We're to go along the main road to Lennet Magna and home across the Common, skirting Randall's Meadow." Susan's eyes shone with excitement. "And, Georgie, Maxwell likes Pudding! He says——"

"My dear Susan," interposed Miss Kennedy, who did not ride and professed to have no interest in the ponies, "*must* we all be treated to a lecture on Maxwell's likes and dislikes in food?" But, behind her glasses, her sharp eyes were twinkling, so she was not really as ignorant as she pretended. She told the school in general that there would be hockey this afternoon for those people who were not riding, and the usual netball for the younger ones.

As they filed out of the refectory Georgie felt someone tug her arm. Looking down—for a very long way, it seemed—she saw the small, string-coloured plaits of Petronella.

"Please, Georgia! I heard what the big girls were saying just now. Can I—can I see the other Australian, please? Where is she? What's her name?"

"You'll see her presently," Georgie said, rather uncomfortably, recalling what Valerie had said. "But she's almost grown up—she's sixteen, and she comes from Sydney, so you're not likely to know her."

"Oh, I might!" cried the child, clasping her skinny little hands. "Mummy and I spent a whole winter there when Daddy was ill in hospital. Our station was in Queensland, but we had to sell up and come to Sydney—and then, after Daddy and Mummy both died, Uncle and Auntie took me to their home in Victoria. So I know lots of places, you see, and I remember Sydney *well.*"

Georgie felt very sorry for her, but did not know what to suggest.

"You can't see Valerie now, anyway," she began, "because she's with Miss Primrose. But——"

She stopped in dismay as Valerie herself came stalking down the corridor towards them. She had removed her vivid garments and was now arrayed in the dark green skirt and light green blouse which all the Grange girls wore indoors in winter, plus a brilliant orange pullover.

"A nice sort of guy I look!" she said angrily, catching sight of Georgie. "Cousin Bunty made me change. Anything for the sake of peace, I thought, but still——!"

"Oh, please," cried Petronella, "are you the girl from Sydney?"

"What's it to do with you?" Valerie began disagreeably, and then she must have relented. Her manner changed to one of friendly condescension. "Yes, I'm from Sydney, and you're the kid from the wilds of Victoria, I suppose. Been over here very long?"

Georgie did not hear Petronella's reply, for some of her own friends came along and bore her away.

"So that's V.P.," mused Susan. "She looks rather sour, I must say—though she must be quite decent really, judging by the way she's talking to young Petronella. Look, they're going to walk round the garden together."

"Oh, please, are you the girl from Sydney?"

"Good," said Georgie, and then began to wonder. *Was* it good? Through the corridor window she could see the strangely-matched pair setting off together, and she had the impression that Petronella was scared and ill-at-ease.

CHAPTER FOUR

THE FIRST RIDE

GEORGIE told Susan about it as they jogged along the main road to Lennet Magna. It was a cold afternoon, but there was no frost and, early as it was in the year, there was something about the sleeping countryside that was like a faint whisper of spring.

"I'm quite sure that if one tried one couldn't pick out three odder new girls than Valerie, Petronella, and dear Catherine! As for Petronella, she really was terrified, Sue. But when I asked her just now if they *had* met before, she said they hadn't."

"What I can't understand is——" But Susan checked herself abruptly. What she wanted to say was that she couldn't understand how Miss Primrose came to have such a peculiar cousin, but it was not a thing she liked to put into words.

The girls rode on. They were well in the forefront of the party, and kept together for two reasons—because they wanted to talk, and because the two ponies, Spot and Pudding, had made great friends during the Christmas holidays at Georgie's home and kept naturally side by side.

It was a big party today. The Grange School was truly growing out of all recognition, but already the "old inhabitants" were learning to accept and even to like the change.

"There'll be inter-school matches pretty soon," said Susan, "and it'll be good for all our sports really—except riding. I don't know what we can do about that."

"Miss Primrose will probably tell us something tomorrow," Georgie answered. "I say, I like Miss Ruggles and Miss Matthews, don't you? I should *think* that having them means that there'll be some more ponies!"

Something shot past them at a tremendous speed,

The three original grooms, Maxwell, Henry, and Harry, had had more than enough to do last term, but now that the school was growing so fast two new stable-hands had arrived. These were friends of the doctor's daughters—a sturdy, capable pair just a little older than the Sixth Form people. Both wished to take up riding-school work on their own, and in the meanwhile they were sharing coaching with Dr. Lake's two girls and had arranged with Miss Primrose to spend their afternoons at the Grange.

They were out this afternoon, but the girls had not spoken to them yet, as they were being taught the routine by old Maxwell.

startling Spot and almost unseating Georgie

"I'm trying *awfully* hard," said Susan, "not to call them the Rug and the Mat."

As they were now coming to open country, they struck off, as they usually did, across a wide expanse of open country which dropped eventually to the piece of land known as Randall's Meadow. As they began to canter something shot past them at a tremendous speed, startling Spot and almost unseating Georgie. It was Catherine Wilkinson on her swift Starbright. She was galloping in a most reckless manner, as of course she had no knowledge of this country, and might have been heading for danger. She looked better in riding kit than in ordinary attire, they were bound to admit, because her clothes were well cut and she wore them with confidence. *But*—she carried a crop and used it, too, very frequently.

"I say!" Georgie turned a dismayed face to Susan. "If she gallops straight across the meadow and tries to go down Randall's Lane, it won't be so good—think of those loose stones. We'd better go after her and head her off. We *can* if we go the short way!"

"Right," said Susan. "Come up, Pudding! Good old Pud!"

Georgie was already cantering ahead of her, taking care to keep Spot under control. Catherine was slowing down as she reached the crest of the hill, but the turf was slippery, and she had ridden her pony too hard to slacken speed at once. Georgie and Susan heard hooves behind them and knew that one of the grooms was in pursuit. Georgie raised her left hand and pointed to the narrow opening in the hedge which was the short cut she had in mind. Catherine, not knowing the locality, was making for a much larger gap, far away to the right.

Georgie and Susan edged their ponies through the opening and waited, ready to warn the reckless new girl when she appeared that the lane leading down to the Grange from this piece of land was steep and dangerous.

"Why doesn't she show up?" Susan fretted. "I hope

she hasn't come off head first into a bush!"

"More likely that Maxwell, or whoever it was, has caught up with her," said Georgie. "I expect we've done the wrong thing, as usual! I say, how rough the meadow looks—I don't think I've seen it in winter before. Sue! Look at that notice over there. Those must be the caves."

Randall's Meadow was flanked at the far end by a rocky hill, which now showed signs of having been excavated. Part of it had been boarded up, with tarpaulin stretched across. There was a large white notice, too far away for them to read.

"It's out of bounds," Georgie said in a wavering tone. "*'Budge,' says the fiend. 'Budge not!' says my conscience . . .*"

"Come on," said Susan, "let's give the fiend a break. After all——!"

After all, it was not their fault that they were here, so near the forbidden territory, by themselves. They had come hither with the genuine intention of warning a new girl . . . So whispered the fiend into two pairs of very receptive ears!

They galloped across the meadow and dismounted a few yards away from the notice, which read:

DANGER! Falling Rock.

Any unauthorized person entering these caves does so at his own risk. F.U.D.C.

"What does that last bit mean, Georgie? As if someone had started to write Fudge and didn't finish," said Susan hungrily.

"Fontayne Urban District Council, I should think," was the reply. "Hold Spot, will you, Sue?"

But Susan, who had lost her jockey cap by this

time, shook her red head decidedly.

"No, I won't. If there's falling rock about, it'll jolly well have to fall on *both* of us! If there were a bush handy, we could tie the ponies to that."

But there were no bushes just here, and as they now saw the other riders filing slowly through the narrow opening in the hedge, it seemed the wisest move to ride back and join them. Catherine was at the rear with Maxwell, who was leading his big horse, Colonel. She was on foot too, leading Starbright, who was in a bit of a lather.

"Put too much of a strain on her, that's what you're doing, Miss Wilkinson. Pulling up so sudden—for all the world like a cowboy spotting Redskins on the skyline! Now up you get—but don't move off. Randall's Lane's steep and tricky, and I'll lead you down the first time . . ."

"Lead me? I've ridden since I was five!" shouted Catherine. She was clutching something in her left hand, and Susan, spying it, called out: "My cap . . ."

"Oh, *here* you are then!" Catherine cried rudely and flung it at her. It didn't reach Susan, but it did touch Spot before it fell to the ground, and he started violently and nearly threw Georgie. She kept her seat by a miracle and calmed her pony, but she could not help flinching.

"Look what you're doing!" exclaimed Judy Thurston indignantly, coming forward. Like her two sisters she was wonderful on horseback, even to the extent of looking quite handsome when in riding clothes. Catherine, ruffled and overheated, was naturally irritated by the other girl's composure and searched her mind for something nasty to say.

"Sorry, I'm sure!" she sneered. "I'd forgotten

that Georgia was the jittery one. But I remember now—Rosalie told me——"

"Ready?" asked Maxwell grimly, and took her down the lane at a very slow walk.

Judy rescued Susan's cap, and Susan jammed it on her wild red hair. Both were careful not to look at Georgie.

"What's this—a mothers' meeting!" called Miss Matthews, who with her friend Miss Ruggles, and Ermyn and Dandy, were bringing up the rear. "If so, break it up and let's get back!"

So off they went, but the pleasure of the ride was dimmed for Georgie. Rosalie had spoken very unkindly about Catherine, but she wasn't, it seemed, above handing school gossip on to her just the same. Georgie bit her lip. It was *too* much to have her former jittery days recalled to her by a new girl!

"I'll never be like the others," she thought in sudden despondency. "I'll never live down the fact that I used to be afraid." For her confidence was far too easily shaken.

The rest of the school happened to be returning from games at the very moment the riding party came home, and stayed to watch the horses filing in orderly lines to the stables. Amongst those looking on was Valerie Primrose, whose face wore a supercilious smile. Georgie remembered that she didn't ride.

Suddenly Miss Primrose was standing with the watchers. She asked Maxwell how they had all got on, and had a pleasant word for everyone.

"Hi, Withershins—go on, then. Clk, clk!" cried Ermyn Mauleverer as she patted the arched neck of her handsome black pony. He stopped dead.

"Well, I don't think much of *that,* Cousin

Bunty!" Valerie said loudly, openly sneering. Her lank brown hair had been too much crimped, and there was a short piece which she had to keep on tossing back, in a most annoying way.

"Valerie," said the head mistress in a quiet voice which few people could hear, "you know that I have asked you to call me Miss Primrose while you're at this school."

"Oh, all right," the girl said off-handedly. "But I still don't think much of a horse that does the opposite from what one says!"

"He's *trained* to!" flared Ermyn, hearing this. "My father has a circus, and this is one of our best ponies. We brought him up! Our trainer and I taught him to do the reverse command!"

"Why, he must be quite valuable," Valerie said, with new respect. And she put out her hand to pat him. The ease with which she did this depressed Georgie still further. Valerie, so Miss Primrose had said, was another person who didn't want to learn riding. Yet here she was, patting strange ponies without the slightest qualm.

Withershins accepted the homage as his due. Ermyn said afterwards that she wished he had given just the teeniest little nip.

"They are all valuable," said Miss Primrose, in a tone that was colder than anyone present had heard her use. "Now hurry up, all of you, but don't skimp your work. Susan, what has happened to your cap?"

"It fell off, Miss Primrose, when we were crossing Randall's Meadow," Susan answered innocently.

"Oh?" said Miss Primrose, looking inquiringly at Maxwell.

"Sorry, ma'am. I knew you didn't want the

young ladies to go there till you'd spoken to them, but one of the new ones made a mistake like——"

"It wasn't a mistake!" cried Catherine, her pride stung by the suggestion. "I was leading the field, if you want to know, and choosing my own way!"

"Hush!" Miss Primrose spoke now in her usual gentle tone. "It should have been explained to you that when girls are out riding they are to obey Maxwell, or whoever is in charge of the party. Randall's Meadow is out of bounds at the present time owing to the rediscovery of some dangerous caves——"

"Oh, I *see!*" Catherine interrupted her without even noticing that she had done so. "Then that was where those two had galloped off to—when Susan lost her cap!"

Georgie and Susan turned scarlet. They knew that their friends were glaring at Catherine for dropping this mammoth brick, but that didn't really help.

"We did"—Georgie's voice squeaked with embarrassment—"go to see the caves."

"As I have not yet referred to the matter, perhaps you didn't know," said Miss Primrose, who was always fair.

Georgie and Susan exchanged glances. This was really horrible, in front of so many people!

"We did know," Georgie said.

"One of the girls told me, and said she'd heard the prefects saying we mustn't go there. And I told Georgie. But we didn't go inside," said Susan.

"Possibly not, as they're boarded up, I believe. Very well, that will do. Those caves were closed when I was a child because they were unsafe, but now they have been opened again and a new part has been discovered. When they are declared safe, we shall go and explore." And Miss Primrose gave her sudden dazzling smile and turned away, and Georgie and Susan heaved thankful sighs. But of course Catherine had to be told that people couldn't go about telling tales like that, and, being tired and cross already, she took her reprimand badly and answered so rudely that she made herself more unpopular than ever.

Her twin was waiting on the drive near the stables, evidently wishing to help to put Starbright back in her box. She waved her hand, smiling, and Georgie thought again how much nicer Constance was than the tempestuous Catherine.

"Come on, come on!" called Maxwell. "Didn't you hear Miss Primrose telling you to look slippy and no half larks?"

The girls smiled at this free translation and, leading their ponies, moved stablewards. Valerie came forward and spoke to Catherine in an ingratiating manner.

"What a fuss they make about nothing! As if you meant any harm! I call it too bad, going off and leaving you alone—*I'll* come to the stables with you! What's your pony's name?"

"Starbright. But you needn't trouble, thank you. My sister's waiting for me," Catherine returned in a lofty tone, instinctively disliking this gushing person. However, Valerie didn't seem to hear this and walked along beside Starbright. Constance, still waiting, had turned her back and, of course, did not hear their approach. Catherine drew the pony aside so that they could pass, but Valerie, not knowing Constance or realizing that she could not hear, suddenly shouted, "Get out of the way, can't you?"

and seized her roughly by the shoulders.

Constance, who had been treated with the greatest consideration, gave a cry of fright, and Catherine fairly sprang at Valerie. Starbright, her reins dragging, side-stepped a little and wondered what to do.

"Leave my sister alone!" hissed Catherine, tugging Valerie's hair. "I think you're horrible! Everyone's hateful here, but you're the worst . . ."

Constance had caught Starbright by this time, but looked quite bewildered—and no wonder, thought Georgie, coming to the rescue.

"Hallo!" she said clearly. "I'll show you where her loose-box is. Bring her along, will you?"

"Oh, Georgie, be nicer to her—she's had an awful scare," protested gentle Anne, leading her own Pierrot in the same direction, but Georgie knew that the best and kindest thing was to make Constance independent.

"Come along," she said calmly, and Constance nodded.

"Which block is Starbright in—A, B, or C?" she asked.

"In A. The middle one," said Georgie, going ahead with Spot.

Susan was already inside the large stable, settling her Plum Pudding for the night. The girls did not feed their ponies or do actual chores at this time of day, as that would have meant a hopelessly late tea and no prep. The stable-work was done in the mornings, but after a ride they all liked to see their ponies "tucked up," as Maxwell used to say.

"That Catherine!" Susan muttered to Georgie as they came out of Block A into the chilly January dusk.

"I know! Words fail me," said Georgie just as

Catherine herself pushed past her.

"All right. Words fail you. Good job too!" she jeered. "All the same, thanks for being decent to my sister. While we're here, and it won't be for long, you can just go on being decent to her—see?" And without waiting for an answer she made a beeline for the house, her shaggy hair flopping as she ran.

"Well!" said Susan. "What next? Honestly, Georgie, she and that ghastly Valerie are a pair. There's not a pin to choose between them!"

But Georgie did not agree. Catherine Wilkinson was certainly a trial, but Valerie Primrose was something far more sinister.

CHAPTER FIVE

DISCORD

NEXT morning Miss Primrose made a short speech. She spoke of the rate at which the school was growing and said that it would in future be divided into three Houses. As the Grange was an old Cavalier stronghold, she and the staff had thought of calling these Houses after three famous Royalists who were said to have made this their headquarters for a time—Lovelace, Falkland, and Montrose.

"We can arrange the details later," she concluded. "We will have an open discussion one evening, and exchange ideas. But now, as the term is already one day old, we mustn't spend more time on this." And she nodded to the senior who was waiting by the piano to play the march which ended morning prayers.

That day passed very quickly, with hockey for the Middle School in the afternoon. The juniors went riding, and Georgie had a quick glimpse of them setting off, Petronella, on dear little Pumpkin, looking very businesslike indeed.

At tea-time Georgie asked her how she had enjoyed her ride, and received a glowing look in reply.

"It's just grand to have a pony again! We went over the hills, and Miss Matthews showed us where those caves are—the ones we mustn't go to. I'm sorry about that; I'm interested in caves. Then we came back by the road, and that's all!"

"Did you tuck Pumpkin up?" asked Georgie.

"No." The tiny pigtails wagged as Petronella solemnly shook her head. "That big girl Valerie, who's helping in the stable, did it for me. But I'd have liked to . . ."

"Helping in the stable?" echoed Georgie.

"Yes. She's always going to," said Petronella sadly.

Georgie remembered something.

"Does she know any of the places you know?" she asked.

"Oh, no!" said Petronella, and promptly dropped the piece of bread-and-butter which had just been passed to her.

"Do you want anything, Georgia?" asked Miss Giles, the kindergarten mistress. She spoke quite pleasantly, because she liked Georgie, but what she really meant was: "I wish you'd go to your own table, because you're upsetting the children, who dilly-dally as it is!" So Georgie had to go.

After tea they did their usual preparation, and then, when supper was over, the Middle School people settled down to hobbies, which they all enjoyed. Those who didn't go in for hobbies could read, or write, or do what they liked. Some people, Georgie amongst the number, were keen on music, and they gravitated to the old upright piano, which bore all kinds of treatment with the utmost composure. Some girls sewed, others made scrapbooks, or swopped stamps, or knitted, and the three Thurstons, who had brought their terrier Bill to school with them again, coaxed him into the common room and passed him round, rather as if he were something nice to eat.

June, the eldest sister, shared a study with another Sixth-former, so she did not stay long in the noisy common room. Before she went, she tried to say something to Georgie but could not make herself heard.

"Sorry, June! Turn the radio down a bit, will you, please, Valerie?" Georgie implored. Valerie, who had no hobbies, was sitting humped up beside her own little portable wireless, which was blaring away at full throttle.

She turned her back on Georgie.

"I like it this way," she said rudely.

"Yes, but——" June hesitated. Then she reached out and switched off the set. Everyone turned to look at Valerie, who merely gave an unpleasant little smile.

"All right—what did you think I was going to do?" she drawled. "Fly off the handle? I'm not Catherine Wilkinson!"

"No personalities, if you don't mind!" said June, who could become very grown-up when she liked. "I was going to say, make the most of Bill, because this is the last term people can keep any pets other than horses or ponies. Sad, but true! You can all see what confusion there'd be if everyone suddenly decided to keep a dog."

Laura Kenton of the Fifth had brought her Peke with her the first term, but she left him at home now. Georgie, who used to exercise Bill in the days before she could ride, patted his pretty head and told him that he had had a longer scholastic career than most dogs, anyway.

"Of course, it's all different now," she said. "But, June, what's going to happen about the ponies? There won't be nearly enough to go round!"

"Well—there'll be more," said the senior. "It doesn't matter telling you people now, because there's to be an announcement quite soon. No, Pam, I don't know how many . . . Yes, it's really true, Dandy—you see, Miss Primrose is getting them from a big riding-school near London, where our horses came from." June, Joy, and Judy were lucky enough to have a pony each, and they were undoubtedly the best riders in the school, unless one counted the circus trained Ermyn, whose performance was always inclined to be showy.

"Goody, goody," murmured Barbara Snow in her usual envious manner. "Now we poor humble mortals who can't rise to keeping our own ponies will have a look-in!"

"Good night, everyone," June Thurston said remotely and went out.

"I think your remark made her feel rather ill, Barbara," said Pam, "and it's had the same effect on me. You *know* you get just as much riding on the school ponies."

"Oh, you and your everlasting ponies!!" sneered Valerie, throwing out her arms and yawning.

"Where *is* this place, anyway, where Cousin B. is getting the new ones?" And, when nobody answered, she pointed one finger at Judy. "You must know, if yours came from there!"

Judy flushed, but answered courteously.

"Bramblemere Stables, Bramblemere, London S.W.—if you really want to know."

"I don't," Valerie said instantly; "I was only being matey. I don't care two hoots where your nags come from—I hate 'em!"

A ripple of anger went round the common room. Georgie found herself trembling. She distrusted this girl more and more.

"If you hate them, why do you help in the stables?" she asked coolly.

Valerie gave her a shrewd glance. "To please Cousin B., of course. She wants me to learn riding gradually and get used to the horses first. She says it's the best way with jumpy people." A slow smile spread across her heavy face. "*You* learnt that way, didn't you?" she cooed.

"Hands off Georgie!" said Susan with admirable self-control. She was a person with many hobbies, of which she quickly tired. Just now it was carpentry, Georgie's brothers having presented her with their discarded fretsaw last holidays. She fingered the book trough she was making as if she would have liked to hurl it at Valerie's head.

"Georgie was *really* nervous," she went on. "She couldn't have patted a strange pony the way you patted Withershins! I think this scared-of-horses stunt is all put on!"

"Go it!" cried Catherine, clapping her hands. "Get on with the slanging match. Then we'll see who'll be the next one to call *me* bad-tempered!"

Several of the girls laughed at this, but most of them realized that they were behaving badly. The trouble was, they didn't know how to stop. It was as if ill-temper and jealousy were in the air.

"Come on, Barbara, let's get on with our practising," Georgie said abruptly. She and Barbara were struggling with one of the Edward German country dances as a duet, and it had been quite fun. Now it became a bore.

"Oh, I'm sick of this thing," Barbara muttered as a hideous discord made them wince. "Why should we bother with it? Mr. Simmons didn't give it us as a lesson!"

She flounced off to join Rosalie Hall and her best friend, Brenda Deacon, who were both knitting themselves very fussy jumpers. Georgie, ruefully putting the music away, caught Constance Wilkinson's eye and received a really mischievous grin. She grinned in reply and wandered across to the twins, who were sitting quite near the table at which Susan and a few other energetic people were working. Constance was reading *Treasure Island*, and Catherine, pencil in hand, was scribbling on a small pad on her knee.

"May I look?" asked Georgie.

"It's a free country," was Catherine's off-hand reply.

Georgie took no notice of her manner, but picked up the pad and saw that this time Catherine had sketched the common room and its occupants—turning all the girls into rabbits! Even so, there were some startling likenesses—that energetic rabbit with whiskers agog could be nobody but Susan, and the bored one, yawning in the corner, was Valerie to the life.

"I don't wonder that you feel you ought to be at an art school," Georgie said sincerely, and Catherine looked at her in an almost friendly manner.

"Well—I know what I want to do, you see, and I can't do it," she explained, voicing what artists have been saying ever since the world began. In her earnestness she forgot to cover up her sketching pad, and Ermyn suddenly pounced on it.

"H'm, you *can* draw, can't you? Draw me!" she ordered forgivingly, and this time Catherine complied. A few strokes of the pencil, a few squiggles for curls, and there was Ermyn on paper, her real self too, and not a rabbit.

"Draw *me!* Draw *me!*" cried several voices, amongst them Valerie's. Catherine looked at her quizzically, no doubt remembering their recent hostilities, but she obediently drew Valerie—not, however, in her plain school clothes, but in a glittering gown with a fan in her hand.

"Why, it's *like* me!" Valerie said with pleasure, patting her hair self-consciously. "Oh, what are you doing? You've spoilt it!"

Catherine had added a pair of bedroom slippers, of the most unglamorous type. One had a hole in it with a toe sticking out!

"Beast!" said Valerie, who was—they discovered now—absurdly vain. "I might have known that you would do something like that. You're not the sort of girl we want in this school——"

"'We'?" queried Pam, in a voice that was dangerously soft.

"Well," said Valerie with a smirk, "I don't want to rub in the fact that I'm a Miss Primrose too, but——"

It was just as well that the bell rang for evening

Valerie Primrose, creeping out of the head mistress's study

prayers at this point, bringing that horrible evening to a close.

"I *say!*" Susan breathed in Georgie's ear as they were on their way up to their bedroom. "Do you know that Valerie actually asked Miss Primrose if she could use her phone? She said she wanted to ring up her mother . . ."

"What happened?" gasped Georgie.

"Miss Primrose said, 'No, I'm afraid not; I can't allow any of the girls to do that. But my secretary will telephone for you if it's urgent.' But Valerie just sniffed. She wouldn't let Miss Eversley do it. Said it wasn't really important . . . I don't know what things are coming to!" Susan said, in such a grandmotherly tone that Georgie burst out laughing.

But her merriment ceased abruptly, for no sooner had they reached Bedroom Thirteen than they all heard that most terrifying thing—the shrill call of *"Help!"*

With one accord all the girls on the top floor and those on the floor beneath crowded on to the staircase, and a moment later Ruth Conway, the head girl, came up to tell them what had happened.

"It's all right. Keep calm, everybody. Two of the ponies have broken loose—the small ponies. Pixie and Pumpkin, I think. The men are hunting with lanterns, and Miss Primrose, Miss Starr, and Miss Briac are all out hunting too. So go back to your rooms, please . . ."

"All right, Ruth, but who called 'Help!' like that?" Pam wanted to know.

"I've no idea," said the head girl. "Now off you go, all of you!"

It was Georgie's bath night, and when she

emerged from the bathroom, warm and cosy in her soft camel dressing gown, she thought of those two little ponies and wondered anxiously when they would be found. There was no one about, so, instead of going straight back to her bedroom as school rules required, she ran half-way down the big staircase and peered through a tiny window which looked on to the stable-yard. She could hear footsteps, and saw torches flashing to and fro.

Then, turning away, she saw something even more disturbing: Valerie Primrose creeping out of the head mistress's study, just after there had been a faint ping like that of a telephone when the caller has hung up . . .

Georgie fled.

CHAPTER SIX

THE OLD ORDER CHANGETH

THE missing ponies were soon found, in the vegetable garden, and everybody breathed again. The Grange composed itself to slumber. Only Georgie lay awake, pondering wretchedly on what she had seen. One couldn't do anything, of course. But one couldn't forget.

"Thursday today!" said Dandy Jones when they were dressing next morning. "I kind of like Thursdays—nice, safe, stodgy sort of days they are, with no frills!"

"Geometry *and* Latin!" sighed Ermyn.

"With four of us going on the Seniors' Ride and the rest playing hockey again," said Pam. "And it's our evening for knitting for the fishermen. I wonder what book Miss Primrose will read to us this time . . ."

It certainly promised to be a very placid day. There were fishcakes for breakfast, and ordinary, rather dull lessons all morning.

"I shall be riding with you this afternoon," Miss Primrose announced after lunch, speaking to the assembled seniors, "because I must make certain notes in connection with the gymkhana. Four Middle School girls are to join our ride—Judy Thurston, Susan Walker, Anne Conway, and Ermyn Mauleverer."

The four chosen Fourth-formers exchanged proud and delighted glances. Georgie smiled her congratulations, but experienced a terrible pang of envy. She was ashamed of this, for of course she knew that she was not nearly such an experienced rider as the four Miss Primrose had mentioned. It was ridiculous to feel so disappointed.

But what was the head mistress saying now?

". . . didn't seem wise for you to ride another pony, Georgia, as you will naturally ride Spot at the gymkhana . . ."

"Miss Primrose! I don't understand," Georgia faltered, feeling that every eye was fixed upon her.

Miss Primrose raised her eyebrows.

"But surely you received a message from Maxwell? Spot appears to have strained his right shoulder. It isn't much, but the vet will be coming to see him this afternoon. I thought Valerie had told you. That is why you will not be joining this afternoon's ride."

Georgie coloured, half delighted, half afraid. So she wasn't a dud! She said as much to Pam as they ran down to the hockey field a little while later, not in so many words, of course, but in a roundabout way which Pam understood perfectly.

"I'm sorry about Spot—d'you think I'll be able to go and give him an apple after hockey? Pam—I'm glad I'm not a beginner any more!"

"Well, you could hardly be *that,* after learning for three terms," Pam said dryly. "But you have come on marvellously just lately. When the Rug—or was it the Mat?—told me yesterday that four of us would be riding today, she mentioned you, and not Susan. Of course Sue's not really used to her new pony yet; I expect that was why Miss Primrose didn't mean to have her today."

Georgie felt almost glad then that Spot *had* strained himself. It would have been dreadful if Susan had been passed over! Then she began to wonder about Pam, who was herself a very good and reliable rider.

"I haven't got a pony of my own," Pam explained, reading her mind, "and a good many of the events at this do in Randall's Meadow are for pony-and-rider."

"There are more ponies coming, from a place called Bramblemere."

"I know," said Pam, "but even so, there'll never be enough to go round!" And she gave her infectious chuckle and dismissed the subject.

Georgie went on thinking about it. Pam was cheerful and matter-of-fact where Barbara Snow had been bitter, but their problems were the same. Because the school was growing, they would both get far less riding because they were not lucky enough to own ponies. Many others, of course, were in the same boat. "I'd have been in it myself," Georgie thought, "if Teepoo hadn't given me Spot!"

But what was the answer? The fortunate few riding less frequently and sharing their ponies? She shuddered. That was unthinkable . . .

"Georgia, must I ask you *again* to go to your place

"Maxwell, where's Spot? Has the vet been?"

on the field? Centre-forward, if you please, and kindly put on this red sash to remind you on which side you are playing!" Miss Kennedy was taking hockey this afternoon, as Miss Starr, the real games mistress, was out with the riders.

Then Miss Kennedy blew her whistle, and play began; but she was a tiresome coach, stopping the game for the least little thing. The girls were not sorry when a deluge of rain put an end to hockey for the afternoon.

"Hurry indoors, all of you! Don't get wet," cried the mistress, and Catherine Wilkinson muttered something about not being made of sugar.

"I can endorse *that,*" Miss Kennedy said coldly. "I may add that I was thinking less of your health than of the difficulty of getting your clothing dried. Hurry!"

They obeyed, streaking across the field at top speed. Georgie made for the stables, determined to find out more about Spot's strained shoulder. She found Maxwell, idle for once and looking rather sour, leaning against the door of Spot's loose-box. It was empty.

"Maxwell, where's Spot? Has the vet been?" Georgie asked in sudden alarm.

"The vet's been changed seemingly, Miss Georgia. I can't make head or tail of it. Miss Primrose never said a word about it to me!"

The head groom was upset. His weather-beaten face, with its grizzled moustache and bushy eyebrows, looked baffled and hurt.

"What do you mean?" asked Georgie. "Spot——"

"You've no call to worry. He's been taken away, you see, to some new-fangled surgery. We've a new vet, that's all. Comes from Lyndhurst way. Miss Primrose, she asked him to come and collect both of them this afternoon. But she never told me!"

That fact rankled so much that it was some time before Georgie could gather what had happened. Soon after the riding party had set off, a horse-transport van had arrived, and the driver had explained that he was to take two sick horses—and he had their names written down and everything: Spot and Mademoiselle—to the new vet's modern clinic on the fringe of the New Forest.

"But Spot isn't really ill! !" cried Georgie. "And what's wrong with Mademoiselle? I haven't even seen her yet this term."

Mademoiselle was kept for Miss Primrose's own use. All the girls were intensely proud of her, though her excitable temperament made her rather unapproachable. Georgie had twice saved Mademoiselle, once from being burnt when her stable caught fire, and once from being stolen, so the spirited mare *should* have been grateful and followed her rescuer like a lamb. But there was nothing lamb-like about Mademoiselle! She would graciously accept tit-bits from Georgie, as she did from the others, but the only real friend she had made was the little donkey, Penelope.

"There's nothing wrong with her," snorted Maxwell. "A course of anti-rheumatic injections—*that's* what she's been taken away for! And Miss Primrose never——"

Georgie wished that Miss Primrose *had* told him. She hated to see him so upset. She decided to go indoors, but paused to ask about Spot.

"How did he strain his shoulder, do you think? He seemed all right yesterday."

"He was all right this morning, miss, but that Miss Valerie Primrose, she was busnacking about in the stables after dinner, and she reported the symptoms to Miss Primrose, who said it must be a strain."

"Well—wasn't it?" Georgie pressed. "You must know, Maxwell."

He shrugged. "I'm getting past it, I am . . . Anti-rheumatism injections! Huh!"

Georgie left him and walked slowly towards the house. She felt disturbed without quite knowing why. Somehow she did not think that Spot was really bad—surely she would have noticed if there had been something wrong? And what did Valerie know about horses, anyway?

"Georgia!"

Here was Matron now, coming swiftly to meet her. Bother, was she late for tea?

"Yes, Matron?" she queried meekly.

"Has the riding party come back?" Matron asked, and when she heard that it had not she bit her lip. "Oh well, it can't be helped," she murmured. "Whoever it is will have to ring up again . . . It's an urgent message, you see, and it would have been so much better if Miss Primrose had been able to take it herself."

Matron sighed and went indoors. She looked worried and was clearly unaware of the rain which had taken the starch out of her flowing cap.

Georgie followed and changed into a frock, as they always did for tea. Susan and Ermyn were still in the bedroom, putting the finishing touches to their attire, but the others had gone downstairs.

"How do you like my new blue velvet?" Ermyn asked Georgie, sweeping an impressive curtsey as she held out her skirt in both hands. She had massed her golden curls on top of her head, and—being an actress to the core—had acquired a grace to match the really lovely frock she wore. It was *too* lovely, of course, for school, but it suited her so well that Georgie could only gasp.

"Why, you look—you look like a daughter of the house in Stuart times! It's beautiful, Ermyn—but do remember that your pen leaks!"

"Grandma Georgie!" Susan said affectionately. "It won't matter, anyway, because the ink and the dress are both blue. Yes, Ermyn, you do look like a Cavalieress. I do wonder which Houses we'll be in."

"I hope I'm in Lovelace," said Ermyn, "because I do!"

"I expect we'll hear more about this House business tonight," said Georgie, when they had chuckled over the little pun; and then they all hurried down to tea.

Miss Primrose, however, did not make any announcements that evening for the simple reason that she was not there. Miss Kennedy took prayers and, comparing notes afterwards, the girls found that they had all thought her manner strained and anxious. Miss Primrose, she said briefly, had been called away on business but hoped to be back quite soon.

"All these upsets!!" Susan said crossly in Bedroom Thirteen. "I've *never* known such a term before. When is Spot coming back, Georgie?"

"I don't know. Oh, tomorrow, I should think. Maxwell didn't seem to think there was much wrong with him——" Georgie paused as someone tapped on the bedroom door, and Pam called out, "Come in!"

It was Ruth Conway. She was still dressed, because the Sixth did not retire until later. In her usual quiet way she asked for Georgie and took her out on to the landing.

"Miss Starr and June and I have just been to the stables to see Maxwell," she began. "There's been some muddle. I suppose Miss Primrose didn't say anything to you about the vet?"

"To me? No, Ruth. What's happened? Is Spot all right?" cried Georgie, thinking of a thousand dreadful possibilities.

"I think so, Georgia. It's not that. It's just—— Well, I'll tell you. Miss Kennedy said I could if I thought you would take it well. Spot and Mademoiselle have disappeared. That vet at Lyndhurst can't be traced. They're not in the telephone book, and the post office says there's no such address."

"Ruth! But Miss Primrose sent for him—at least——"

"Well, did she?" Ruth countered. "Earlier this evening Evans, the real vet, came here intending to examine Spot. He said Miss Primrose had sent for him. He didn't know anything about treatment for Mademoiselle."

"But I don't understand," said Georgie. A cold, sick feeling was sweeping over her, making speech difficult. "Ruth—horses can't just vanish. Can't you get in touch with Miss Primrose, and——"

"No," said Ruth sharply. "We can't. We don't know her address."

For a moment they stared at one another, the tall head girl and the Fourth-former, who was still unconsciously clutching her hairbrush. Ruth, usually so tranquil, looked troubled now, and Georgie could not hide the dismay that filled her heart.

"Ruth, I'm frightened!"

The words burst from Georgie's lips, and when she saw Ruth's start, she wished she could recall them.

"Georgia, don't say that, please. You're one of the old originals, you know—one of the old soldiers who never die!" A faint smile lit up Ruth's face. "Perhaps we do feel a little—worried—but we must put up a good show for the sake of the new people, and the Grange. Now you must go back to the others, and when they ask you why I wanted you, say that it was to ask about Spot."

"All right, Ruth."

"If they keep on asking you, perhaps you'll have to say a bit more. Don't tell them anything that isn't true. But try not to show that anything is wrong."

"Then something *is,*" said Georgia, clutching the banister rails. She couldn't—she *couldn't* lose Spot!

"Something may be." Ruth was non-committal. "Go back now and try to sleep. Perhaps everything will be cleared up quite soon."

Yet it seemed to Georgie, looking out of her window that night, that not only were Spot and Mademoiselle in danger, but some mystery was shrouding the whole school.

CHAPTER SEVEN

IN THE DARK

JUST after breakfast next morning Ruth spoke to Georgie again.

"It's all right," she said. "I'm sorry I worried you last night. The new vet—Mr. Harcourt—rang up to say that Mademoiselle and Spot are very well and will be returning the day after tomorrow."

"That'll be Sunday!" Georgie pointed out.

"So it will—how funny of him to make that mistake. He said he hoped we hadn't been anxious —he's only just arrived in this part of the world, which is why he's not in the phone book. He wanted to speak to Miss Primrose, of course, but Miss Eversley passed on the message. So that's all right!"

"Yes," Georgie echoed, "that's all right!"

But somehow it wasn't, and both girls knew it.

By this time a certain restless uneasiness had taken possession of everyone, and all sorts of wild rumours were flying about the various forms. Little Nancy Andrews, of the First, actually stopped Georgie, when they met in a corridor, to ask her if Miss Primrose really had bought a ranch somewhere and gone to live on it! The Fourth, however, took a gloomier view. They were convinced that more long-lost cousins had cropped up, and she had gone to collect them and would shortly bring them to join Valerie at the Grange.

If Valerie Primrose felt any concern for her relative, she hid it extraordinarily well. She was the only girl to go on as usual. She had been put in the Fifth Form, where she was the despair of Miss Waite, who was less strict than Miss Kennedy but perhaps even more fussy about things like punctuality and tidiness. Valerie was very slack. She did not work or show any sign of interest in books. She tried to avoid wearing uniform, putting on dreadful frilly blouses instead of the plain, well-cut green ones which the girls wore every day.

When reprimanded by her form mistress or the prefects, she merely shrugged. "Cousin B. never told me not to!" was her trump card, and she used it the other way as well when it suited her. Maxwell asked her not to spend so much time in the stable, as—being a novice—she needed constant watching. "Miss Primrose said I could be here whenever I liked!" was her answer to that.

There was a ride that Friday afternoon, only a short one, on Lennet Common. Georgie, ponyless now, had to wait till the others were mounted, but Judy Thurston proved unusually helpful. She asked her sister Joy to lend Georgie her pony, Daring, who was a blood brother of Judy's own Punch.

"Gosh, he's much too quick for me!" Georgie told Susan, in alarm, but Susan only laughed.

"He's a goer, but he knows where he's going—and it'll be jolly good practice for the gymkhana. We may have a Paul Jones, when you might get landed with simply anything on four legs! Let's see how he gets on with Pudding."

But Pudding was missing Spot. It was touching to see him looking this way and that, obviously wondering what had become of his friend.

"Have you heard when Spot's coming back?" Georgie asked Maxwell as the cavalcade crossed the old stone bridge on the Common. "I'm sure they won't really be brought back on a Sunday."

The old groom shrugged his shoulders, an austere look on his face.

"Your guess is as good as mine, Miss Georgie. A proper mystery it is to me—and to Mr. Evans. A fair slap in the face it was to him! 'Tisn't as if Miss Primrose made mention of a new vet, even when she said goodbye. Back she came from her ride," he said grimly, "and out came Matron to say there's a message for her. Twenty minutes later out she comes, changed into ordinary clothes and all. 'Maxwell,' she says, 'will you get me the car? I've got to go away sudden-like,' she says. So I got the car and," he finished dramatically, "she upped and offed, with never another word!"

But now, hearing a commotion several hundred yards away to the right, Maxwell "upped and offed" himself, and Georgie and Susan trotted after him to see what was happening.

The stream which divided the Common narrowed suddenly a short distance below the bridge, and as the winter had been such a dry one the banks were hard and firm. Ermyn had set Withershins to perform a water jump—a thing strictly forbidden in this place, where the width of the stream varied day by day. He had done it, of course, as she had known he could—and now Rosalie was urging Catherine to do the same.

"Go on! Not scared, are you? I'd try it myself, only Flora—the pony I've got today—is much too fat and slow. Go on—let's see if Starbright is as marvellous as you think!"

"She's marvellous all right, as you know. You've seen her often enough at home! But that stream's about six inches too wide," said Catherine coolly.

"Yes," said Ermyn, giving Starbright a speculative glance. "'Shins only just did it——"

Catherine flushed, thinking that Ermyn was casting a slur on Starbright.

"Oh, I don't know!" she muttered stubbornly. "We might have a stab at it, anyway . . ." and she rode back, to give herself a good start.

Maxwell, coming on the scene just then, ordered her sharply not to attempt the jump. But Catherine was determined by this time, and off she went.

Starbright got over all right—but only just. In scrambling up the farther bank she dislodged her

There she was, in shiveringly cold, muddy water

rider, who fell with an ignominious splash right into the middle of the stream. Poor Catherine! This was a bitter moment for her, especially when Rosalie, Brenda, and Barbara all burst into peals of laughter.

There she was, in shiveringly cold, muddy water, her feet slipping away from her whenever she tried to climb up the bank, her face and hands plastered with slime and her hair oozing horribly.

"Pull her out, somebody!!" Georgie called out, as Maxwell was busy capturing Starbright. Ermyn would have done so if Withershins had been calmer, but the noise of the splash had excited him. So Georgie dismounted, though she did not want to (it meant mounting again, and Daring *would* dance at her!), and went to give the discomfited Catherine a hand.

"I can manage, thanks!" said the victim furiously, but she had to give in. Her muddy paw reached out, and a moment later she was up the bank.

"I'll have to report you for this," was all Maxwell could trust himself to say as he brought back Starbright. But Catherine only tossed her head.

"Do!!" she said. "I don't care—and in any case, Miss Primrose is away."

"Huh!" said Ermyn. "Miss Kennedy's deputy head, though, and she'll be livid. You'll see. You are a goat; you might have had Starbright down."

Catherine flushed angrily and made some sharp retort, but Miss Ruggles had come on the scene by this time, and ordered the little group to collect and catch up the rest.

"I wouldn't be in *your* shoes for a million pounds!" Rosalie told Catherine, rather smugly, as they rode away.

"Her shoes are better than Georgie's, anyway!" giggled Barbara. "Georgie'll be fined for removing half Lennet Common!"

Georgie grinned, but it was an effort. Her feet felt cold and clammy, and her jodhpurs, which happened to be new, were stiff with mud as well.

"Cheer up, Catherine!" bellowed Susan. "Miss Kennedy never says much . . . It's what she *doesn't* say!"

The remainder of that ride was uneventful, and all too soon—for Catherine's peace of mind!—they were back at the Grange.

"Now," said Miss Ruggles, who had had a bad scare, "we are going straight to Miss Kennedy!"

"I'll go by myself, thanks," said Catherine haughtily, and Georgie, afraid that the girl would bring even more trouble on herself, was glad to be able to point out quickly that Miss Kennedy was emerging from the side door.

Catherine gave her a glance which, if not grateful, was not actively hostile. Then she stalked forward.

"I've got to report myself——" she began, but Miss Kennedy waved her aside.

"Not now, not now," she said rapidly. "Girls, how late you are! Will you please go straight to the big hall? At once!"

Everyone stared in dismay at the mistress, who had never before appeared so agitated. Georgie had a sudden dreadful idea.

"Miss Kennedy—has something happened to Miss Primrose?"

Her form mistress looked at her curiously.

"Yes, and no," she replied in a hesitant manner quite unlike her usual crisp, decisive one. "Miss

Primrose will be away for several days. Mrs. Gaunt, her cousin, has come to look after the school in her stead."

Georgie, after that first moment of shock, realized that Miss Kennedy was badly shaken herself. The knowledge was disturbing. Looking at Susan, she saw that they had the same feeling.

"I didn't know the Kenpot *could* be ruffled, except in a fierce sort of way!" Susan confided as they ran indoors. "Seeing her like this makes me feel all wriggly inside."

"I know," said Georgie. "I feel as if I'd come to slay a dragon and found it was only a lizard. Why should the Kenpot be so upset?"

"Because she wants to be deputy head and can't?" But Susan's tone showed that she did not really believe this.

"No," said Georgie. "I think she's just as much in the dark as we are. Mrs. Gaunt! Oh, I wonder what she'll be like? What lots of relations Miss Primrose seems to have all of a sudden!!"

But even then she failed to guess that Mrs. Gaunt was Valerie's mother. That fact did not dawn upon any of them until, filing into the great hall, they saw the obnoxious Valerie on the dais with a short, thick-set woman with a face like pink leather and rather staring blue eyes. She had untidy white hair and the mouth of a bully.

"Hurry up!" she rasped. "Into your places with you! Now—I'm your Head until Miss Primrose comes back. She's in London on business, and while she's there she's making a little holiday of it. She'll be back some time soon. Her orders are that you'll behave yourselves and get on with your work and not give me any trouble. Carry on now in your usual way. What should they be doing, Valerie?"

"They change and have tea now, Mum."

"Mum!" A little ripple of horror ran round the listening girls. That one short word had told them everything. Valerie's mother (who, as they were told later, had married twice, which explained why she was Mrs. Gaunt instead of Mrs. Primrose) was now in charge of the Grange, with Valerie as her lieutenant!

"Off with you now!" said the stranger, clapping her hands as if she were a sultan in the Arabian Nights, and they a batch of slaves. "You don't need to change. Go and have your tea." She smiled at Valerie. "And we'll have ours!!"

The situation was bordering on the absurd. Several people had to stifle nervous giggles, while others felt as if they were in the grip of some fantastic nightmare.

"I say, Georgie!" Catherine Wilkinson spoke in an urgent whisper. "I've simply got to change— I'm soaked. Your feet are too, aren't they?"

"Of course we'll have to change," said Susan; "we always do after riding. She doesn't understand."

Soon, however, she found that it was she who did not understand. As she and Georgie and Catherine and some more of the riding party made for the stairs, they were called back by Mrs. Gaunt herself, who was standing in the doorway of Miss Primrose's study, obviously waiting for her tea.

"Come down, you girls! Didn't you hear what I said? No sneaking off by yourselves! Go and get your tea, and afterwards I'll tell you what to do."

In startled silence they turned towards the refectory, which was already in an uproar. Miss

Kennedy and some of the other mistresses sat at their own table at the far end of the room. Their blank faces showed that they too were utterly bewildered.

Nobody ate much tea. Even Susan gave up after two sandwiches and a bun. The Fourth-formers stared at one another miserably.

"What happens now?" asked Judy. "Do we do our prep. in riding kit, or what?"

"You sit tight," said Pam grimly, "and don't move till you're told."

"I feel kind of winded." sighed Ermyn, "like some performing tigers in my Pop's circus. Their trainer got ill and another man tried to take them on, but no. Those tigers just couldn't thole him!"

"What's *thole?*" cried several voices, and Ermyn looked wise.

"It's the Scottish for 'bear'," she informed them.

"Goldilocks and the three tholes," Susan murmured, just to tease her, and Ermyn shook her golden curls.

"No, not like that! I can't thole Mrs. Gaunt, see?"

It was, of course, at that very moment that the new head mistress—for so she styled herself—opened the door and marched into the refectory. Her hard blue eyes grew harder still.

"You with the yellow hair," she said, "what's your name? And you, who tried to go upstairs when I'd told you not to?" They gave their names quietly and calmly. "Speak up!" she commanded, and then, as they did so: "Don't shout! I will have order. Go to your rooms and begin preparation, in silence, mind. And in future no talking at meals. If you can't keep civil tongues in your heads"—with a sidelong glance at the crimson Ermyn—"you'd better not use them at all."

And when Miss Ruggles presently came in with some query from the stables, Mrs. Gaunt would not let her address Miss Kennedy.

"From now on," she said, "and you can tell the grooms as well, this place is being run by my daughter and myself, and don't you forget it!"

Sadly and wearily the girls filed to their places to do their prep. Georgie's feet were still heavy with mud, but her heart was heavier still.

"Oh, Sue," she whispered, "I wonder what the house is feeling! It must think that history times are back again and the Roundheads have captured the Grange!"

CHAPTER EIGHT

THREE IN EXILE

GEORGIE woke early next morning with a heavy, thick feeling in her throat. She thought at first that it was depression—and she, in common with all the other Grange girls, had certainly good reason to be depressed!—but very soon she realized that she had caught a cold. Those wet feet!

Dismally she dived under the pillow for her handkerchief and heard a muffled croak from another bed. Someone else was in the same boat.

"Who's that?" Georgie whispered, and the reply came wafted on a sneeze:

"Be! Catheri'd. Id's o'dy a code!"

"Colds?" said Susan, waking up. "They can't be! They take three days to come."

"They needn't," said Judy; "they can come on in a few hours if one sits about in wet boots, which Georgie and Catherine both did. Tough luck—on a Saturday too!"

"I won't report mine," Georgie declared firmly, adding, as cold victims usually do: "It's *nothing!* It'll be over in a few hours."

But she and Catherine both barked at breakfast, and looked so heavy-eyed that Matron soon spotted what was the matter. Mrs. Gaunt and Valerie had not appeared. Rumour had it that they were using the study as a breakfast room!

"I'm popping you both into the sick room," said Matron when she had put her thermometer away, "not because you're very ill, but because we don't want the colds to spread. There's another girl in there already, but you must keep away from her. You won't be there very long, any of you."

"Who is it, Matron?" asked Georgie in an anxious tone. She was glad to know that she wouldn't be alone with Catherine, and naturally hoped that the third person might be of a peaceful type.

"One of the juniors. She's been having nightmares and seems rather upset. Petronella Smith," said Matron. "Fetch your pyjamas and washing things and come with me."

"I won't," said Catherine.

"I beg your pardon!" Matron's eyes grew wary.

"I'm not going to leave my sister. You know she can't hear. She needs me!" Catherine insisted.

"Does she?" asked Matron gently. Her window was half open, and she motioned Catherine to look down at the broad garden path which ran below. A little knot of Fourth-formers was chattering there, and in the centre was Constance, looking quite at ease as she lip-read what the others were saying.

Catherine turned crimson and said no more.

The sick room was on the floor below Bedroom Thirteen, and a light, pleasant place. Two rooms had been knocked into one, and now it contained eight beds. In the farthest of these huddled Petronella, her eyes enormous in her small white face. She glanced up in a frightened manner as the door opened, but when she saw Georgie her expression changed to delight. She leapt out of bed and came running towards her.

"Now, now!" said Matron. "Back you go. These girls have colds and you are not to go near them."

Petronella accepted this meekly; she was, it seemed, a meek little girl. She said, "I don't mind as long as they're *here*."

"Don't excite her," said Matron in a low tone as she gave Georgie and Catherine a loathsome draught apiece. "And don't ask her about Australia—she doesn't like talking about it."

How funny, Georgie thought; Petronella hadn't minded at all that first afternoon. But ever since she had spoken to Valerie she had seemed more silent. "Poor little scrap," thought Georgie, and wished that she had one of her friends with her instead of the glum Catherine!

"Atishoo!" said Catherine at that moment. "What are the others doing? What usually happens on Saturdays?"

"It used to be a lovely day," Georgie answered, "but of course, now that Miss Primrose's away, it may be quite different . . ."

It was! A letter from Susan, brought in by Matron at the end of that long, long day, read as follows:

Dear Georgie,

You haven't missed much! Two of the maids gave notice this morning and walked out, and now Cook has gone too, and WE are having to do all the chores. Everybody is ramping, but not aloud, because we get punished. I am being punished now, for breaking a tea-cup while washing up—that is how I'm able to write this. Oh, Georgie, what can have happened? Doesn't Miss Primrose know how awful Mrs. Gaunt is?

Here followed a row of smudges.

Sorry about these [the letter continued], but I had to hide this epistle as the Enemy approached. Have just seen Ermyn, and you'll never guess the latest. THE STABLES ARE OUT OF BOUNDS!!!

Come back soon. We are all desperate. I had a parcel from Mummy today—chocs—and that Valerie has wolfed the lot. And she was nasty to Constance—pushing her and telling her she was in the way—so Anne and Dandy locked her up in the stationery cupboard, but she shrieked like a banshee, and now *they* are locked up—in the little music room.

I will carry this about till I see Matron, who will give it to you. I wonder what *she* thinks? The staff won't speak about Ma Gaunt, but they look as if they could say a lot.

Sue.

P.S.—One bright spot—the ponies are being fed properly. I crept out to see.

Georgie read this letter three times, trying to grasp its contents. She must have lost her colour, for Catherine asked sharply if anything were wrong.

"Just about everything, I should think," Georgie answered, and would have left it at that, for Catherine was not a friend and Petronella was only a junior, and a new one at that. But Catherine's long brown hand reached out for the letter and, before she realized what she was doing. Georgie had let her have it.

Catherine displayed more tact than she had shown hitherto, for she read the scrawled pages in silence though her face flamed when she came to the part about Valerie and Constance. She folded the letter carefully and gave it back to Georgie.

"Well, if that's the way things are," she said, "we can do as we like, I suppose, as long as we don't get caught. I used to do that at my other schools, but—it seemed a bit different here."

"It *is* different," said Georgie earnestly. "This is just a bad patch. Miss Primrose will be back soon, I'm sure, and then you'll see. You'll love the Grange as it really is."

"Ah!" said Catherine, a mocking gleam in her dark eyes. "But will it love me? All right, Georgie, don't worry—I shan't blow it up with gunpowder just yet! By the way, I'm sorry I played you up—that time when you and Susan went into the caves."

Georgie could not know that this was the first

voluntary apology which Catherine had ever made to anyone except her twin, but she did sense that it was an effort, and she accepted it at once. Then a faint sound at the other end of the room made her look in Petronella's direction, and she saw that the little girl was sitting up in bed, a hopeful look on her face.

"Georgie, if you're going to tell each other stories, *can't* I come nearer and listen?"

"But we're not, Petronella, and you don't want to catch our colds, do you? You can tell us one if you like—you can talk properly, and we can't!" and Georgie gave a terrific sneeze as if to prove her point.

Petronella giggled. "I can't tell stories. I thought you were going to tell one about the caves. Oh, that reminds me—my Daddy used to tell me a story about a cave he was playing in when he was a little boy, and a piece of rock fell down and blocked it up, and he couldn't get out. And he was there for hours and hours with nothing but chewing-gum to eat. He found a sharp stone and drew animals on the walls with it."

"Did he like animals?" Georgie asked gently. "Used he to ride when he was a boy?"

"Yes!" cried Petronella. "Whenever he got the chance. He didn't have a pony himself, but there was one he always called Sheltie, and he used to ride him for miles and miles. I was going to call mine Sheltie, but you see he turned out to be Turkey instead . . ."

They let her chatter. Catherine had found a pencil and paper and was idly sketching the view from the nearest window. Georgie, drowsy and yet conscious of a gnawing worry, lay down and answered the child from time to time without really taking in what she was saying.

When Matron brought in the supper tray she, too, looked grave and preoccupied.

"Is there any news of Miss Primrose, Matron?" Georgie asked at once.

"No." Matron was busy administering a horrible dose which had to be taken before meals. Her hand shook slightly. "I expect she will let us know soon when she means to return."

"My feet are cold," said Catherine. "Can I have another hot bottle, please?"

Matron hesitated. "I'm afraid not," she said. "Mrs. Gaunt feels that we are using too much hot water, and—er—thinks we shouldn't use hot-water bottles. So I have brought you three pairs of bedsocks."

They were new and beautifully knitted. The girls took them wonderingly.

"Oh, Matron, they're yours!" said Georgie.

"My dear, I knitted them for the next church bazaar, but they were made, after all, to be used. But I'm afraid Petronella will find hers much too big!"

They all laughed when Petronella stood up in bed, looking rather like Puss in Boots, with bright pink bedsocks on her tiny feet.

"You're nearly well, young lady!" said Matron, but at that Petronella wilted and dived between the sheets.

"I'm not," she said. "I feel awfully, awfully ill. I don't really think I shall make old bones!"

"Eat your supper," said Matron. "You'll be in the sick room for another day at any rate."

"I'm beginning to think we're all in the best place," said Georgie, but Matron's sense of loyalty forbade her answering that.

The colds were at their height next day, and Georgie and Catherine were glad not to have to get up, especially when they saw snowflakes whirling past the windows. The bedsocks had kept them cosy and warm, and Matron managed to bring them an extra blanket each. They lay and listened to the Lennet church bells, thinking what a very peculiar Sunday this was going to be.

"Matron, what time do you think Mademoiselle and Spot will be brought back?"

"I don't know, Georgia. I think it's a strange idea sending them back on a Sunday. Most vets wouldn't take out a van unnecessarily."

"Matron—how's Constance?" Catherine asked abruptly.

"Very well indeed. Everyone's practising Morse on her now. You started that, didn't you, Georgia? It's certainly caused some amusement. Constance is a very quick-witted person, isn't she?"

Catherine nodded. "That's why it was such hard luck she got ill," she murmured, and lapsed into heavy silence which was more gloomy than sullen this time. Georgie was quite glad of Petronella's company, remote though it was.

That Sunday wore on slowly, and the snow fell steadily till nightfall. No transport van appeared. Matron, coming in at last to say goodnight, brought a message from Maxwell. Georgie was not to worry. No news was good news, etc. The new vet had not telephoned, but no doubt he knew that they would not expect the horses to be returned while the roads were so slippery.

"Wouldn't have hurt him to have rung up, just the same," growled Catherine, and Georgie, who had been thinking the same thing, said quickly that of course it was all right, and there was sure to be a message tomorrow, anyway . . .

There was no more snow, but frost glistened on the window panes next morning and the trees flashed and sparkled in the winter sunshine. Because all were such keen riders, the three girls in the sick room groaned when they saw the icicles.

"I suppose nobody's allowed to ride on a day like this," said Catherine. "I wouldn't take Starbright out."

"No, we shouldn't be likely to go when the roads are as bad as this . . . I say," said Georgie, drawing a deep breath, "my cold's gone. How's yours?"

Catherine's, too, had taken flight, much to Petronella's distress. But her respite was over in any case, for when Matron came in she told them all that they must get up. Mrs. Gaunt thought it was time they joined the others.

The two Fourth-formers were quite ready to do so. They were tired of inaction now they felt quite well, and Georgie wanted to hear from Susan and the others what really was happening in the school.

They had breakfast in bed and then dressed. They were to go straight down to their forms, so Matron had said, and Georgie and Petronella had to wait for Catherine, whose belongings had a habit of eluding her. Georgie leaned out of the open window. The air was ice-cold but fresh and dry, and so still that every sound carried.

"I can hear a horse being led," observed Catherine. "Who is it? Can you see?"

"Just," said Georgie. "Why, it's Starbright! But she won't be going far."

"How do you know?" cried Catherine, rushing to the window.

A gasp of amazement was jerked from her

"Well, look who's leading her! Valerie," Georgie pointed out, "and she can't ride properly yet. That's why she's putting in so much time in the stables—to get used to the ponies. Starbright may have got cramp, and Valerie's walking her to the gates and back. She—— *Oh!*"

A gasp of amazement was jerked from her as Valerie, evidently believing herself unobserved, swung lightly across the unsaddled Starbright with the ease of lifelong practice and then rode out of sight.

CHAPTER NINE

REBELLION

GEORGIE sat in an unusually cold form-room, staring at a page of French irregular verbs. All around her sat angry-looking girls doing exactly the same thing. Even Miss Briac, seated at her desk at the far end of the room, looked grave and aloof—not at all like her usual cheerful self.

Mrs. Gaunt, it appeared, had objected to the girls' usual method of learning French. There must be no more acting, no more interesting story-books and magazines, and no more songs. Verbs must be learnt instead, in silence.

Georgie, wondering wearily if *s'asseoir*, that arch-enemy, would ever come to terms, let her thoughts wander for a few moments. This was Tuesday—the day after she and Catherine and Petronella had left the sick room. That meant that for the last twenty-four hours she had been sampling life at the Grange under the command of Mrs. Gaunt.

It was worse than any nightmare. It was—well, she could hardly believe, even yet, that it had happened. In appearance Mrs. Gaunt was like her daughter, with the same overbearing and yet petulant expression, but in manner she was much harder and sharper, with none of Valerie's laziness. Valerie, Georgie was glad to see, bore no likeness to Miss Primrose. Poor Miss Primrose, to have such cousins as these! Yet it was not of Mrs. Gaunt's hostile attitude to the school that Georgie was thinking, or of the nasty bullying way she had addressed the three as soon as they left the sick room. What had upset her more than anything had been Petronella's terror the day before.

Catherine had, quite understandably, flown into a temper when she heard that Valerie was riding Starbright. She said she was going to tackle Valerie in front of everyone, and ask her what she meant by pretending she couldn't ride, and then she was going straight to Mrs. Gaunt to demand point-blank why the stables were to be out of bounds. She would have said a good deal more, only she and Georgie both saw that Petronella was in tears.

"Don't—*don't* make them angry!" was all the child would say, her face pale with fear and her small frame trembling. "Don't let her, Georgie! Oh, don't, don't!"

But she would not answer when Georgie asked her what had frightened her like this. Catherine had gruffly advised her to stop blubbing and making such an ass of herself, and Petronella had apologized, but had begged her again not to anger Mrs. Gaunt and Valerie.

This painful little scene came between Georgie and the verbs, and with puckered brow she remembered how Petronella had wilted when she asked her what Mrs. Gaunt had done to cause such fear. She had quite meant to tell Susan about it, but there was no time till they were going to bed, and by then Bedroom Thirteen was in a ferment. The Grange—so public opinion declared—was going to the dogs!

"Yes, Georgia? Your lesson is perhaps not clear?" came Miss Briac's voice, and Georgie realized that she must have sighed aloud. She stood up.

"It's not the lesson, Miss Briac. But nothing is clear!" she said, while the other girls held their breath. "We don't even know whether Mademoiselle and Spot have come back from the vet's place yet, and—and nobody will tell us anything about Miss Primrose. Don't *you* know when she's coming back?"

"No, Georgia," the mistress said briefly. "As for the two horses—no, they have not returned. But there is, I think, no cause for alarm. The roads are still bad between here and Hampshire."

The words were reassuring, but the stiff, unnatural tone was not. Miss Briac was the jolliest person imaginable as a rule.

"Do you know what I think?" Pam asked a group at break. This, by the way, was now spent in the big hall, although Miss Primrose had always liked the girls to get a breath of fresh air on the drive. "I think the staff will leave in a body if this goes on. Mrs. Gaunt was frightfully rude to the Kenpot this morning. I didn't hear what it was all about, but the Kenpot seemed to get much taller, and blue sparks came out of her eyes!"

"We shall leave in a body too," said Susan, tossing her red head angrily. "I'll write to Mummy tonight in prep. There are heaps of other schools with riding. Let's find a decent one and get our people to send us to it!"

"Now, now!" said Mrs. Gaunt, bustling into the hall. "I want six for kitchen fatigues——" She glanced round at the silent girls. *"You'll* do," she said, pushing Susan towards the door. "And you, and and you, and you and you—and *you!"* she finished up, glaring at Georgie, who had been gazing at her in a speculative fashion, trying to puzzle out how any relation of Miss Primrose could be so thoroughly disagreeable. "You can get the coal in," Mrs. Gaunt told Georgie, almost as if she had read her thoughts. "It'll do you good after lolling about in the sick room."

The chosen six marched off to the kitchen regions. They did not mind housework in small doses and would have helped cheerfully if there had been a domestic crisis at any other time. But to be herded into the kitchen like this, and ordered about by this cross-faced, loud-voiced woman, stirred them to rebellion.

Georgie staggered backwards and forwards with coal. Susan and Judy peeled a mountain of potatoes, and the other three—Third-formers, as it happened—were told to make a bread-and-butter pudding with some stale loaves. They didn't like to say that they had no idea of how to make one even when supplied with the proper materials. Instead, they did their best—and their best was fearful beyond words!

Mrs. Gaunt must have suspected that it might be, because she came into the refectory while this pudding was being served, although she and Valerie were going down to the village for lunch.

"Wasting good food!" she exclaimed, seeing the untouched plates. "I can't have this. Eat up your pudding at once!"

"It looks ever so nice!" chimed in Valerie, with a coy smile.

Susan made a tiny movement, but subsided when Georgie frowned at her. Catherine, however, had leapt up before anyone could stop her and was offering her plate to Valerie with exaggerated courtesy.

"Do, *do* let me persuade you to try a piece—the wee-est little crumb!" she mocked, her dark eyes glittering so fiercely that Valerie gave a little affected scream and stepped back.

"Mum, stop her—she's being rude to me!" she whined, and Mrs. Gaunt swung round on Catherine. At the same time she caught sight of Constance, who was sitting next to Georgie looking white with the strain. She could not lip-read in a scene like this and had no idea what Catherine had said.

"You twins—you can each eat up your own pudding *and* that of your two neighbours," Mrs. Gaunt grated triumphantly, and had the satisfaction of hearing Catherine plead:

"Not Constance, please, Mrs. Gaunt—she'll be ill; she hates puddings, anyway—and she didn't *do* anything."

But the mistress had her way, and the Wilkinsons had to stay at table long after the other girls. Constance *was* ill, and Catherine, almost sobbing with anger, drew a very ugly picture of Valerie, showing up all her defects.

"I shall put it in her room tonight. If she hadn't yelped like that, we'd never have had such an awful punishment. I hate her, so there!" she said furiously, glaring at Georgie, who happened to see her finishing her drawing. It was early afternoon, but the girls were all hanging about the common room. There was no riding. The road surface, so Mrs. Gaunt had given out, was still too bad. And she considered the weather too cold for hockey.

"Well, I hate her too," returned Georgie, "so you needn't look like that. We all feel just as awful as you do—except it was too bad that Constance got punished." She glanced sadly round the room. "I don't feel that this place belongs to us any more. Oh, Sue, what is going to happen?"

Susan, from her favourite perch on the window-sill, shrugged helplessly.

"It's this stable business that gets me," she said. "If only we could see the horses we'd feel better. It's tosh about the roads being bad—look, the drive is quite soft again now."

"You know," said Georgie, "I feel like a prisoner; and yet free, in a way, to do things I'd never have done when Miss Primrose was here. I don't see why we should be loyal to a head mistress who treats us as Mrs. Gaunt does. From now on I shall be like those people in the Bible, who did that which was right in their own eyes!"

"Yes, but, Georgie, they *did* find themselves rather up a tree," Anne reminded her timidly. "Honestly, breaking rules isn't going to help a bit . . ."

"Listen, Anne, you were a Third-former till this term, and being moved up doesn't give you permission to boss us about!" snapped Barbara, who was—as usual—on the fringe of the group.

"Anne isn't bossing, and what she says is perfectly

true," flared Susan, "only—at the present moment I feel like Georgie. I want to break out!"

"Well, why don't you?" jeered Rosalie Hall. Everyone was scratchy this afternoon. "All this nattering about what you will and won't do! Why not *break* out?"

"Yes, let's dare them to do something," said Brenda Deacon, quick to take Rosalie's cue. "'Mm, I know! Go to the caves in Randall's Meadow and bring back a stone or something to prove it."

"We'd be spotted first thing," Georgie objected, but Susan, ready to accept the challenge, had her answer ready.

"If we got over the wall at the bottom of the vegetable garden we'd drop into Randall's Lane. We *could* do it. I'm ready if you are, Georgie!"

"Can I come too?" asked Catherine.

Georgie and Susan exchanged glances. They were old and tried friends and badly wanted to discuss things together; but Catherine, wild and somehow rudderless, must be considered as well.

"Right!" said Georgie. "I don't know what'll happen if we're caught, but what does it matter?" And, glad to have something definite to do, they slipped down to the cloak-room to fetch their coats, and then, keeping cover, went softly into the wintry garden.

"It's a relief to have something to do," said Susan, "even if it's only a kids' stunt like this. Georgie—*where* can Miss Primrose be? I wish we could catch a glimpse of Maxwell . . . But Valerie will be in the stables. She always is."

"I must know soon what has happened to Spot," Georgie said restlessly as they dropped over the wall into the lane.

When they reached the meadow, which they did quite soon, Catherine ran on ahead to find the caves. Georgie called after her to be careful, and then she and Susan walked more slowly, talking over the dismal changes at the school.

"Have you written to your people yet, Sue?"

"No, because I remembered they're just off to Brittany, to compare the Breton language with the Welsh—or the Irish, or something!" Susan was always vague about her father's important work, which involved a study of dialects. "Anyway, it didn't seem fair to prick their balloon just now, poor pets!"

Georgie laughed. "You're awful, Sue. But—I felt the same in a way. There's my family picturing us settling down to another lovely term, and I couldn't upset them so soon. They wouldn't believe it, probably. I don't think I do myself."

"Do you mean you don't believe it's happened, or you don't believe that things are as they seem?" Susan asked shrewdly, and Georgie jumped.

"I don't know! But there *are* queer things going on, apart from Valerie's pretending to be a beginner when she can really ride. I feel quite creepy whenever I think about it—come on, race you to the cave!"

It was a dead heat, and when they entered—very cautiously—they found Catherine looking happy for the first time that day, crouching on her knees, drawing on the cave walls with some chalk she had found in her pocket. Families of sprightly animals grew under her clever fingers, and then she spoilt the effect by drawing another picture of Valerie, much worse than the last.

"There—conceited creature! How I loathe her!" she cried passionately. "I loathe everything!"

A chilly wind blew round the caves. It was the time on a January evening when everything suddenly seems very cold and sad.

"Let's go back," Georgie said abruptly. Anne had been right—deliberately breaking rules wasn't really the answer.

"Right!" said Susan, in a tone which showed that she had reached the same conclusion.

So they walked back to the school, in silence mostly, as the dusk gathered in the trees and the pale sun sank behind the hills. There was a faint afterglow, and as they drew nearer they saw the Grange as it must have appeared to many people during the long years—a friendly, kindly, welcoming house, despite its dignity. Its familiarity struck Georgie and Susan, and even Catherine gazed at it with something like awe.

"It must have been pretty good," she sighed, "the way it used to be."

"A house," said Georgie, almost angrily, "is only brick and stone and mortar. We *don't* owe it loyalty any more . . ."

"Of course not! From now on we're *tough!*" cried Susan, all the more fervently because she knew so well how Georgie was feeling. "Come on, nip through this french window—there's nobody about."

But as they skirted the entrance hall they glanced at the beautiful staircase and held their breath. For someone *was* about—someone, whose bearing as well as her attire belonged to a bygone age, was coming slowly towards them.

CHAPTER TEN

SUSPICION

FOR a moment the three girls stood silent, and then Susan gave a short laugh.

"Well, we *are* a set of owls! It's only Ermyn," she said, and the slender blue figure on the stairs paused to sweep her a curtsey.

"*Only* Ermyn? Huh!" snorted the owner of the name, continuing her stately progress. "Nay, varlets, know ye not that I am the Lady Ermyntrude Fitz-Primrose, come back to haunt yon upstarts till they flee?"

Georgie and Susan chuckled a little. Ermyn in this mood could be irresistible. She had actually let down the hem of her blue velvet dress, so that it almost swept the ground, and her curls had been massed on her head again, with just two hanging across her shoulders. Lace taken from some other garment was draped across her shoulders. Catherine's fingers searched her pockets automatically for a pencil.

"Dash, I left it in that cave," she said crossly, "and it was a good one too."

"You used chalk in the cave," Georgie reminded her.

"I know. But I tried my pencil first, because someone else had been using one . . . Oh, well, I'll have to go back for it some other time."

"No," said Georgie.

Catherine and Susan both stared at her, and she

coloured a little.

"We *can't* break rules the whole time, and do all the things we shouldn't. I thought it didn't matter, but it does. It isn't fair on the house," she said earnestly.

"On the *house?*" echoed Susan. "What on earth do you mean? It's not as if Miss Primrose were here."

"No, but the Grange is still the Grange," said Georgie. "I realized it just now, when Ermyn was pretending to be one of the people who lived here long ago. All sorts of things have happened here—big, important things, some of them—and—and——"

"You mean," said Susan helpfully, "that it's sort of up to us? Even with Ma Gaunt in charge?"

Catherine made an impatient sound, but Georgie nodded, sighing deeply.

"I do mean that. I wish I didn't. We needn't be angels, but let's be ordinary and not do things we've been specially told not to. I think it matters all the more, somehow, because Ma Gaunt is——"

A hand came out and clutched Georgie's arm in a painful grip.

"What did you call me?" demanded Mrs. Gaunt in a thick, angry voice. She had obviously overheard, so Georgie did not reply. Mrs. Gaunt shook her, and then her attention was caught by Ermyn, who was now standing at the foot of the stairs.

"You dressed-up little doll!" she sneered. "You know I've told you not to waste time changing. Still, never mind. I want you to come to the stables with me."

"What did you call me?" demanded Mrs. Gaunt

"But—but it's dark!" burst out Susan, and the woman snapped at her.

"So I am aware! Come on, you."

The others would have loved to follow, for the stables were out of bounds now, and they had not seen any of the grooms that day. But Miss Kennedy, passing just then, told them briefly to wash their hands and come to the refectory.

"But it's too early for supper, and we've missed tea," said Susan in surprise.

"You've been out, I can see," Miss Kennedy mentioned coldly. "Well, there is no need to discuss that now. Tea and supper are being combined in future, and you are just in time for it."

She began to walk away with her usual haste, but Georgie, for once forgetting her shyness, sprang after her and barred her way.

"Miss Kennedy! Do you know where Miss Primrose is, or when she's coming back? We can't go on like this, can we? Oh, please don't think it's just curiosity," she cried. "It's just that we can't understand——"

"Hush!" said Miss Kennedy, standing very still. Her face flushed slightly but her manner remained the same—restrained and somewhat sarcastic.

"I don't believe you to be curious, Georgia. Merely foolish," she said, "to imagine that I can discuss the situation with you. Of course I can't do that. But I may say that the answer to both your questions is No. Now please go to your meal."

Georgie thanked her and followed Susan and Catherine to the refectory. All the girls, except Ermyn, were sitting there in gloomy silence, dealing with the weak, purple-looking cocoa and thick slices of bread which had been distributed. Before she took her place Georgie crossed over to Anne Conway and told her frankly that she had been right.

"We went to the caves as we said we would, and we're not sorry," she declared, "but—I don't expect we'll go again."

"Genius," said Susan loftily, "never repeats itself, anyway! Golly, is this *all* we're having to eat?"

Thickly cut bread, with a scraping of butter and fish paste, accompanied by lukewarm cocoa, is not an inspiring meal for anyone. But the girls tackled it with praiseworthy determination, perhaps because they were really hungry. They were not thinking solely of themselves, however. Susan voiced the thoughts of them all when she muttered something about wishing she knew how the horses were faring.

"We'll ask Ermyn when she comes back," said Pam.

But when Ermyn did walk in towards the end of supper, murmuring some excuse before she sat down and helped herself to the unappetizing fare, nobody asked her anything. For one thing, she looked so tired and worried—Ermyn of all people, who never let anything get her down!—and for another, the mystery now enveloping the school seemed to press round them, stifling them, like a fog.

Georgie looked up suddenly, and her hazel eyes met Ermyn's blue ones. Each read in the other's face a fear that was all the more intense because its cause was unknown. Georgie thought suddenly, "They *shan't* spoil the Grange! Whatever it is they're up to, we won't let them get away with it . . ."

But what *were* they up to? Or was it, after all, sheer supposition? Miss Primrose was away on

c

business, and her cousin, Mrs. Gaunt, was running the school. That was the position in a nutshell —and yet *why did Valerie pretend she couldn't ride?*

"Feel all right, Georgie?"

"Yes, thank you, Sue."

"Well, I don't!" was the heartfelt rejoinder. "I really am starving this time. I'm thinking of walking down to the village to buy sandwiches at the inn."

Susan looked as if she meant it, so in low tones her friends pointed out the disadvantages of such a journey, and the unpleasant music to be faced on her return.

"Oh, all right," she said at last, "I'll give up. I'll starve. But I'd like to see inside an inn—there'd be darts, I expect, and—other people to talk to. Strangers, I mean. People who don't know anything about this place!"

"Look out," said Ermyn nervously. "Walls have ears, and all that. I agree with Sue. *I'd* like to talk to a stranger too. There's something"—she dropped her voice—"secret going on. I wasn't allowed to go into the stables, and I couldn't catch a glimpse of Maxwell or anyone. But I had to stay in the yard with Ma Gaunt, and Valerie brought Withershins up to me."

"Go on," said Georgie tensely, while the other gasped in surprise.

Ermyn brushed some mud from her blue velvet dress.

"I did feel a loony," she said, "having to ride in *this* thing! And it was almost dark. I can't think what it was all about. Ma G. said they were keen to know how I managed to mount, as he waltzes about rather—as you know!"

Her friends laughed. Of all the horses and ponies at the Grange, Withershins was the best trained in showmanship. Naturally very intelligent, he obeyed Ermyn and her father implicitly, but he used his judgment with other people. He did "waltz" sometimes when he wished to discourage a would-be rider. But with those he knew to be Ermyn's friends, and especially with the timid and inexperienced, he was as gentle as the little donkey Penelope.

"Who's been trying to ride him?" Georgie asked in a low voice.

Ermyn shot her a quick glance.

"Just what I wondered. I asked, but they didn't answer. They don't know that you saw Valerie on Starbright. Anyway," she said, dimpling into a smile, "I've got them puzzled!"

But at this point the dismal tea-cum-supper came to an end, so it was not until bedtime that she was able to explain what she had done.

"They know all about the Reverse Command, so I couldn't diddle them there. But 'Shins is awfully sensitive round his ears, and I pretended to pat him, and kept on jabbing him with the buckle of my watch strap. And that made him dance, in spite of what I was saying."

"Oh, Ermyn! That was cruel!" cried Anne.

"It does sound beastly," said Catherine, and Ermyn flared up at once.

"Yes, and I thought the same last time I rode with you, and you kept on using your crop! I didn't jab hard—I wouldn't hurt 'Shins, or any pony, for the world! But it was to save him," she said furiously, "from being stolen—like your Starbright!"

There was a sob at that, but it did not come from Catherine. Constance had been sitting up in bed, lip-reading the conversation. Now she buried her face in her hands, and Catherine, her face dead white in its frame of untidy black hair, turned fiercely on Ermyn.

"Now look what you've done! Saying a thing like that, out of the blue——"

"Shut up, Catherine," Pam said briefly, as head of the dormitory. "We'll talk about Starbright later. Don't you see that Ermyn made Withershins behave awkwardly so that *they* shouldn't try to ride him?"

But Catherine was trying to tell Constance that Starbright was all right and was not in the least bit likely to be stolen . . .

"Don't be too sure," murmured Ermyn, not unkindly.

"Tell me after lights-out, then," said Catherine, turning away so that her sister should not read those words.

Nine unwontedly solemn people were lying in bed, not bothering to talk, when Matron came to say goodnight. She too looked harassed—all the staff did nowadays—and did not comment upon the unusual silence. Constance was quite composed now, but Catherine's voice was sharp with misery when she spoke next, waiting for Matron's footsteps to die away.

"Well? What about Starbright?"

"I don't know," Ermyn said at once, "but I couldn't see her. I told you I wasn't allowed in the stables, but I did sort of crane my neck and peer a bit, and though I could recognize some of the ponies —Pudding, and Pierrot——"

"Oh, thank goodness!" burst from Anne.

"—and Flora and Colonel," Ermyn went on, "I couldn't spot Starbright. And don't forget, Valerie can ride her!"

"I see what you mean. Thank you," Catherine said coldly, and lay down, pulling the eiderdown over her head.

One by one the girls fell asleep, but Georgie lay taut and still, her eyes wide open in the darkness. Her brothers Rough and Tough had once deliberately mixed up three jigsaw puzzles, and it had needed boundless patience to sort them out. But at least all the pieces were *there,* she thought wearily, whereas she was now trying to fit together mere fragments.

There was a moon tonight, and after a little while Catherine went to the window to look at it. Georgie, who was nearest, silently offered her a dressing-gown, which she put round her shoulders. Her face, in that weird light, was grimly set.

"Catherine," Georgie whispered, "we don't *know* about Starbright. She may be perfectly all right. As far as we know, she hasn't been carted off like Mademoiselle and my Spot."

"You think I'm making a fuss about nothing!"

"Of course I don't! I'm trying to cheer you up, but you're absolutely uncheerable!" snapped Georgie.

"Sorry. Only I hate it when Con gets upset. She's rather a lot to put up with." Catherine hesitated and then told Georgie something which explained her odd behaviour. "She's always been the good one. I'm awful! It's because I climbed up a cliff we'd been told not to go near, and got stuck, that she came to rescue me and fell into the sea and got the illness which has made her deaf. If only it had been me! I'm the one who ought to be punished——"

"Well, so you are," said Georgie, really sorry for her now. "Seeing her deaf must be worse than being like it one's self. Anyway, she's getting better, isn't she?"

"They thought she would if we went to a healthy open-air school. Rosalie's mother was always telling our mother how wonderful it was at the Grange. It did sound wonderful, too—Miss Primrose was frightfully decent about my having been sacked from those other schools for climbing on the roof, ringing the fire-drill bell, and putting mouse-traps in people's beds . . . She said I wouldn't have time to do those things here, because we were always occupied with riding and games and acting and so forth. But it's all horrid now, and Constance and I are *miserable* . . ." And Catherine's voice trailed off into an angry little whine.

"Well, the rest of us aren't exactly jumping for joy," Georgie remarked dryly, and then she remembered that she was an old Grangeite, and Catherine an extremely new one.

"Nip back to bed now," she said with sudden authority, "and don't let's worry till we have to. Let's keep out of trouble, that's all. And—be decent to people; everyone, I mean, not only Constance. Try . . ."

"Can't promise that," said Catherine darkly, "but I won't use my crop unless I need it." She smiled in the moonlit darkness. "Can't I even draw that nasty picture of Valerie?"

"Well, not too nasty. But it needn't be nice," said Georgie, so feelingly that they both laughed softly before Catherine tiptoed across to her own bed.

CHAPTER ELEVEN

THE LENNET STEEPLECHASE

THE next day began, as days did begin now, very drearily, with no stable chores, no prayers in the hall, and only some very thin porridge, made by Mrs. Gaunt herself, instead of the cheerful breakfast which Miss Primrose wanted everyone to have.

The girls were growing restless. As they went to their various form rooms one could feel the uneasy atmosphere deepening. Meeting Valerie in one of the corridors, Georgie was surprised to see that she too looked gloomy and worried.

"I don't know what *she's* got to grouse about," Susan muttered when Georgie told her this.

"Oh. I do," said Anne. "Ma Gaunt's just been biting her head off. It was when she was giving out the post just now. Some silly argument about an Australian flower . . ."

Georgie had a sudden idea that this might be important—though why she did not know.

"Which flower?" she asked quickly.

"Waratah," Anne answered, staring. "Pam's cousin in Australia mentioned it in a letter she got this morning, and she asked Judy what it was like. You weren't there, I suppose. Well, Judy didn't know, so she looked across at Ma and Valerie, who were standing by the letter-board—you know how they always snoop at post time!—and they both spoke at once. Ma said it was a sunflower, and

Valerie said it was a kind of mimosa. And then they glared at each other, and Ma blew Valerie sky high!"

"I *wish* I'd seen that," said Susan yearningly. "Which was right, anyway?"

Several of the girls who had witnessed the little scene began to laugh.

"Neither," said Catherine. "I saw that scared kid Petronella in the distance and asked her—and she says it's a red flower!"

"But of course it is," said Georgie, remembering now that she had seen a picture of it in a book at home. "It's like a bright red globe artichoke. How funny——"

"Valerie didn't think it was funny," Catherine murmured, as she dived into her desk for the necessary pencil. Ten more seconds and an absurdly doleful face, all too recognizable, was adorning her rough note-book.

Constance, whose desk was next to her sister's, leaned over to look at the drawing, which was being admired by Catherine's immediate neighbours.

"Better look out," she said in her clear little voice, "Miss Kennedy will be coming soon, and she looked grim at breakfast . . ."

Georgie nodded. She had noticed that too. All the staff had looked strained just lately, but this morning Miss Kennedy in particular seemed less approachable than ever. The girls felt rather apprehensive as she entered the room, and they dutifully rose to their feet. But she seemed calm enough now, though her thoughts were obviously far away.

"We'll concentrate on chords and circles today," she said; but concentrate was the one thing that nobody could do. Miss Kennedy realized this, for she suddenly stood up and dictated two riders for them to work out. Then, with a brief "Good morning, girls," she swept out of the room, a complicated figure left unexplained on the blackboard.

"But there's twenty minutes to go before French begins!" exclaimed Judy, who didn't like people to do unusual things.

"Let's try the first rider," said Pam.

So for a few minutes there was much thought and pencil-gnawing, and a few plaintive groans. Then Ermyn sprang up excitedly. From her desk she had a good view of the drive.

"Look, everyone! There's the Kenpot in her outdoor things, handbag and all!" she shouted. "I'm sure she's going to leave!"

With one accord the girls rushed to the window and gazed incredulously at the familiar figure, tall and angular in a long winter coat, walking swiftly up the drive. Susan threw up the window and leaned out.

"Miss Kennedy! Don't go!" she yelled, and several other voices joined in. "*Please* don't go!"

They forgot now what a dragon she could be. At that moment she was a trusted friend who was deserting them. She heard their cries and turned quickly, laying her finger to her lips. But she did not come back.

"It's no use," Georgie said huskily. "She can't stand it any more. She doesn't want us to make a row in case *They* come out . . ."

"Come on, everybody," Pam said briskly, as befitted a captain. "Chords and circles for all we're worth. Somebody clean the board."

Catherine was nearest to the blackboard, so she picked up the duster and rubbed out the figure Miss Kennedy had drawn. Then she hesitated. She ought, of course, to have gone back to her desk and struggled with those riders again, but temptation was too strong. She picked up a lovely fat piece of chalk and began a lightning sketch. She frowned, rubbed it out, and tried again . . .

Georgie watched her. It fascinated her to see this girl draw, because Catherine was a real artist, with far more ability in this direction than Miss Moon herself. Miss Moon, the art mistress, had passed exams which perhaps Catherine Wilkinson would never pass, but she lacked the spark of genius.

Catherine drew a galleon in full sail, a couple of mermaids, and a flying horse. Intent on her work, she seemed unaware that the girls were watching her. The flying horse became a pony with a star on his forehead. She hesitated and then drew a half-moon beside the star.

"Is he yours?" asked somebody, and Catherine shook her head.

"That kid Petronella said she had one with the Turkish flag on his forehead," she said carelessly, and drew a string of ponies.

"Oh, Catherine! What a funny little one at the end—he's like a sausage on legs!" cried Anne. "And he'd trip on a tail as long as that."

"It's all out of proportion," sniffed Rosalie in her most superior fashion, and that got Catherine on the raw. She shrugged angrily.

"As if I didn't know! I'm copying a creature someone had drawn inside those caves—you saw it, Georgie! The same pony—if it is a pony—over and over again, like a frieze!"

"No, I didn't see it," Georgie said slowly, while something seemed to echo in her mind. Petronella's voice . . .

"I had a pony called Turkey." Petronella had said that, but it was something else that Georgie was trying to think of now. And in a flash it came to her. It was Petronella again—Petronella in the sick room, terrified of something, refusing to speak of Australia, yet eager to know about the Fourth-formers' adventure in the caves. "My Daddy was playing in a cave when he was a little boy, and a piece of rock blocked it up, and he was there for hours and hours. He found a sharp stone and drew animals on the walls. He didn't have a pony, but there was one he called——" Georgie came to a full stop, racking her brains.

"Catherine! Oh, you've rubbed it out—do please draw that queer pony again," she begged. "There wasn't a name written beside him by any chance? And—was he drawn with a stone?"

They were all staring at her, but she didn't care. She was on the track of something which might affect the destiny of the whole school.

"I saw the pony she means!" cried Susan. "Yes, it was sort of scratched in stone, Georgie—wasn't it, Catherine?—after someone had made some streaky marks with pencil. And there was a name——"

"Yes, there was," said Catherine positively, her quick mind grasping the fact that Georgie was desperately in earnest. "I think it began with an S."

"Then——" Georgie stood up, aware of a queer choky feeling which made it difficult to speak. "I think that proves something—I'll tell you later," she stammered. "But we must catch the Kenpot before she goes away. She may be able to help. Oh, Sue! *Can* we catch her?"

In the instant of silence which followed her frantic

question the girls made up their minds to trust her. They were agog with questions, but realized that these must wait.

"We'll chase her," cried Susan, "on horseback! Come on! And if we meet anyone who says 'Out of bounds'——!" She ran to the door.

"Sue—Sue, come back," said Ermyn. "Where has the Kenpot gone? To the station?"

"Oh, I think so. I'm sure she has," gasped Georgie. "She lives in London, I know. Quick, *quick!*"

Some people, like Judy and Pam, would have liked to ask questions even now, but they soon found themselves addressing an empty room. Georgie and Ermyn, and most of the Fourth Form, had fled to the stables in Susan's wake.

They ought to have been prepared for what they found there, but they were not. All those empty loose boxes, and that dismal air of neglect! So many ponies were missing. Withershins was still there, and so were all the small ponies and the donkey Penelope. Flora and Polly were there, but Starbright was missing. Georgie and Susan rushed to see what had happened to Pudding, and almost cried when they saw his speckled, friendly face regarding them with mild surprise.

"Where's Starbright?" cried Constance in distress.

"Where's Pierrot?" gasped Anne.

"Mind out, everyone," Ermyn ordered crisply. "I'm going to ride 'Shins bareback, to save time."

Susan decided then to ride Pudding in the same way, though she had never done so before. She had often ridden her other pony, Black Agnes, without a saddle, but then she had had her for a long time and knew her every move.

"Come on, Ermyn," she said. "Cheer up, Georgie—we'll catch the Kenpot for you—dead or alive!" she added, her love of drama getting the better of her.

"Oh—*will* you?" rasped another voice, and the girls spun round in dismay. There, standing by the stable door, her arms grimly folded, was Mrs. Gaunt—and beside her, pallid with apprehension, lurked Valerie.

Catherine tried to push past them, but Mrs. Gaunt caught her by the arm and shook her furiously.

"Let me *go!*" shouted Catherine, losing her temper. "I've got to fetch Constance—she's looking for Starbright——"

She broke off abruptly, and even Mrs. Gaunt had to step aside as Ermyn brought Withershins out. He was excited and made some prancing steps in their direction.

"Look out, Ermyn," said Susan, bringing Pudding to the door. And Georgie, watching, felt a pang of envy so keen that she could have wept. Ermyn and Susan could ride forth on a daring attempt to catch Miss Kennedy, but she, having lost her pony, was powerless.

It was like that other time—that dreadful day in her first term at the Grange, when the stables had caught fire. She had felt this sickening helplessness then, as she watched Teepoo, the African girl who had proved such a good friend, set off riding little Penelope, to give the alarm . . .

Penelope!

For once obeying an impulse as wild as any of Susan's, Georgie went up to the small brown donkey. She had ridden Penelope before, just for fun, copying the way Teepoo had ridden—sitting well back. She wondered frantically what she should do if Mrs. Gaunt tried to intercept her, and then she saw that the hard-faced woman was fully occupied with Susan and Pudding. Ermyn had already broken away and

The hard-faced woman was fully

was trotting up the drive. So when Georgie swung herself across Penelope's brown, plushy back she set off unnoticed.

Suddenly a frightful shriek rang out, and Georgie's heart leapt in fear. But she patted Penelope's neck and urged her on. Something had happened just ahead of her, and when she came to the gates she would see what it was . . .

She thought that Ermyn must have been thrown,

though this was very unlikely. But in another moment she saw that it was worse than that. Ermyn, on Withershins, had, quite accidentally, ridden Constance down.

"Georgie!" Ermyn was white to the lips.

occupied with Susan and Pudding

"She was just ahead and I called, 'Get out of the way!' I forgot she was deaf—I forgot! And now——"

Now Constance, that gentle, good-tempered person who had gone to the gates to look for Starbright, was lying in a silent, huddled heap.

Georgie heard running footsteps, and saw that Catherine, Anne, and some others were coming to see who had given that scream. Ermyn, clinging to

Withershins's mane with one hand, was staring down at Constance.

There was no need for everyone to stay. Georgie dug her heels into Penelope's sides, gasped out a word of encouragement, and set off at a funny little trot.

How slow it seemed, after riding Spot! And yet Penelope was covering the ground far more quickly than Georgie could have covered it herself, even if she could have kept up a good running pace. In her anxiety and impatience, however, it seemed like one of those nightmares when one is in such a violent hurry and yet powerless to move. She wondered why Susan did not overtake her, and then, as she found herself meeting a sudden spate of traffic, she stopped wondering about anything except the state of Penelope's nerves.

Ah, here was the Common! Setting off along the broad path which Miss Kennedy must have taken if she intended going to the station, Georgie patted Penelope and told her to relax. The donkey had not liked the noisy cars and motor cycles, for she led such a quiet, happy life these days, helping the gardener to keep the school lawns smooth, but she had behaved beautifully. Now, however, she really galloped, to Georgie's mingled relief and discomfort —because she found it very hard to keep her seat.

There was the old stone bridge with its low parapet. Georgie imagined herself falling over this into the stream where she and Catherine had come to grief a few days ago. But it was deeper here . . . She must dismount and lead Penelope! But she conquered her fear, because donkeys are notoriously obstinate and Penelope might refuse to gallop again.

As they drew near Lennet Magna and its little

wayside station Georgie began to think that this was, after all, nothing but a wild goose chase. Why had she assumed that Miss Kennedy was going by train? In any case, a car might have picked her up—or perhaps she had reached the station already and was even now steaming away to London, or anywhere.

She pricked up her ears. There *was* a train! Oh, how awful it would be to reach the station just in time to see that tall, angular figure disappear into a No Smoking or a Ladies Only . . .

Penelope was tiring now, but it didn't matter. They were at the station, and—Georgie let out a war-whoop!—there was Miss Kennedy crossing the yard.

The mistress turned in utter astonishment, but before she could speak there came the sound of the train stopping, and then——

"Miss *Primrose!*" cried Georgie and Miss Kennedy in one breath.

Miss Primrose, the only passenger to leave the station, came slowly towards them. She was pale and her right arm was in a sling. She said in bewilderment, "But how did you know I was coming by this train? I didn't know myself till three hours ago!"

Georgie waited politely, but found that Miss Kennedy was at a loss for words. So, clinging to Penelope's topknot, she plunged into breathless speech.

"Miss Primrose, some ponies are missing and everything's simply awful! And—and are you sure it's Valerie who's your cousin? Because *I* think it's Petronella!"

Even then, with her heart pounding and the world rocking wildly around her, she noticed that while

Miss Kennedy started in amazement Miss Primrose didn't seem surprised at all. But before anyone could speak again Susan hove into sight, skimming over the ground on Pudding.

Susan's face was as white as junket, and her freckles looked quite dark. She slid to the ground and moistened her dry lips with the tip of her tongue.

"Will you come, please?" she said to Miss Primrose, whose presence she seemed to take for granted. "And Miss Kennedy? Oh, Georgie, Ma Gaunt and Valerie are running away, and we all think that Constance is dead . . ."

CHAPTER TWELVE

DONKEY DAY

"ISN'T it funny," Georgie remarked thoughtfully some weeks later, "how an accident, or an illness, can make people forget other things, even though they're frightfully important really?"

She was addressing her family, as it happened, who—in common with many other parents, brothers, sisters, uncles, aunts, and friends—had come to the Grange on the day of the Lennet Gymkhana.

Mr. and Mrs. Kane and Peter understood what she meant, because they always did. But Rough and Tough, those boisterous twins, were teasing Susan about her book trough, which she had begun so hopefully and had later turned into a bird table, and Uncle Archie and Aunt Milly, who had not visited the school since the pageant last summer, were exclaiming to Ermyn about all the new faces they saw.

"Really, Georgie," said Geraldine, the Kanes' priggish cousin, who spent all her school holidays with them, "you're only repeating what you've learnt over and over again in maths—that the greater includes the less! Of *course*, a horrid accident makes everything else seem small!"

"Gerry Holden, if you talk about maths today, something'll probably happen to you that *won't* be an accident!" Susan burst out. But she had grown more tolerant lately, so the words were accompanied by a reluctant grin. "Anyway," she added, "Constance Wilkinson—the girl who was hurt—is much better now. She's going to be quite all right. That's her twin over there, talking to Ermyn."

Georgie glanced across the garden and noticed, with a shock of surprise, that Catherine looked quite good-tempered and bright. But then she *had* improved. When Constance had been taken to hospital, everyone had expected that the fiery Catherine would wreak vengeance on Ermyn. But exactly the opposite happened. Gay, confident Ermyn was so badly shocked by the accident—the first she had ever caused in all her riding career—that Catherine put herself out to assure her that it was not her fault but just a misfortune which might have happened to anyone. The other girls, struck by this unexpectedly sporting attitude, became much more friendly towards her, and now her outbursts of temper were becoming quite rare and she was settling down. Constance wrote to her twice a week from the London nursing home to which she had been moved, and always sent little messages to the members of Bedroom Thirteen.

It was the twenty-eighth of March, a school holiday, known for lack of a better name as Donkey Day.

This was in honour of Penelope, who had on that date in the previous year carried the message that the stables had caught fire. To celebrate the occasion Miss Primrose had invited all the girls' families to lunch, so that they could go up to Randall's Meadow afterwards and watch the gymkhana which had been arranged. There were a few outside competitors, just to make it more exciting, but the girls themselves had done a good deal of the organizing, under Maxwell's watchful eye.

Gerry glanced approvingly at the clear blue sky and the pale sunshine which sparkled in the budding trees.

"I'm glad the weather decided to co-operate," she said graciously. "Of course I shouldn't be here but for that burst boiler at St. Monica's, which forced the Head to give us a week's holiday! I don't know how the Lads wangled their exeats, I'm sure. Georgie, what *has* been going on at the Grange? I had one wild letter from you, two crazy postcards from Aunt Milly, and the Lads began some utterly fantastic yarn in the car this morning after we'd picked them up. They must have got hold of the wrong end of the stick somewhere. I mean—head mistresses simply don't *get* kidnapped!"

Georgie laughed. She felt so happy today that she could put up with Gerry's maddening way of talking, as if her St. Monica's were the only sensible school in the world.

"It's only just over two months since it happened," she said, "and already we're beginning to wonder if it ever did. Miss Primrose wasn't exactly kidnapped, though—she—— Oh, I'd better tell you from the beginning."

Aunt Milly gave a little scream.

"Oh, my dears, such a dreadful affair! Poor Miss Primrose!" she moaned. "Will she ever recover from the experience, do you suppose?"

Georgie kept a straight face—Aunt Milly was very kind, in spite of her silly, fluttery ways—and quietly remarked that the figure now crossing the lawn with Ruth Conway seemed in perfect health.

"But her arm isn't quite all right yet, so she won't be riding Mademoiselle today," she explained. "The Rug—Miss Ruggles will be doing that. She'll be competing with some of the seniors, and Judy and Ermyn in a jolly stiff jumping event."

"Georgie," said her cousin in a winning tone.

"What, Gerry?"

"Merely that, while we all know that human beings aren't nearly as interesting as horses, we'd rather like to hear about the bogus Head and her dark deeds! It sounds," said Gerry, "so *exactly* the sort of thing you would get mixed up with."

"Why," said Rough at this point, "from all we've heard it seems just as well that Georgie *was* in it up to the neck. After all, she solved the mystery—she pieced the thing together, without a single clue——"

"Oh, I had a clue of sorts," Georgie put in modestly, though she gave her brother a look of gratitude. "The clue was the pony called Sheltie, whose portrait Petronella's father had drawn in the cave when he was a boy. (The caves are safe now, so we'll all be able to look at them when we go up to Randall's Meadow for the gymkhana.) Oh, Mother—Spot's in marvellous trim! He——"

"Darling, I *am* glad," said Mrs. Kane, "but I can't help feeling that Gerry's right. If you could just talk about human beings for ten, or even *five,* minutes——!"

Georgie joined in the laugh against herself, and as they all walked round the sunlit garden she did tell them the story they wanted to hear.

"It was the Conways' Uncle Gordon who began it," she said, "by bringing a photographer friend here last summer. He took masses of photos of the school and the stables, and even of Penelope; and Uncle Gordon, being a journalist, wrote an account of the Grange to go with them. And the photos and story were sold to an Australian magazine, which, eventually, turned up at the home of Petronella's foster parents.

"Petronella," she went on, warming to her tale, "is an orphan. She was living with an oldish couple called Parfitt, who were very kind to her, but she'd no idea that Mrs. Parfitt had once been nannie to her father, when he was young and lived in England, and spent his summers with his cousins at the Grange. Petronella didn't know she was a Primrose. Her father had taken the name of Smith long ago, because of some family bother—I don't know what it was, and it doesn't matter. Anyway, he changed his name when he went to settle in Australia.

"When the Parfitts read that article they thought—as they've explained since then—what a shame it was that Petronella should never see the Grange. So they decided they'd send her here to school, even though they didn't like to tell Miss Primrose who she was.

"But," said Georgie dramatically, "someone else saw those pictures as well!"

"I should think quite a lot of people did, if they came out in a magazine," remarked Tough, who was always literal.

"Georgie means the Gaunts," said Susan loftily.

"They saw a copy of this Australian magazine lying about somewhere in London, and concocted a plan for getting hold of our best horses and ponies, and *selling* them! Mrs. Gaunt isn't a widow, by the way. Her husband did the actual planning."

"Oh dear, oh dear!" twittered Aunt Milly. "It sounds like a film—one of those dreadful sensational ones that Archie and I never go to see . . . Go on, my dear! Tell us the rest."

"Well, they decided to pretend to be Australians," Georgie said slowly, trying to simplify the story as much as possible. "They found out what they could about the Primrose family, even that Miss Primrose called herself 'Bunty,' and made Valerie pose as a cousin. It was just too bad for them that Petronella arrived the same day."

"Gosh, yes!" breathed Rough. "What happened? I wonder Valerie didn't bolt there and then."

"But she didn't know who Petronella was. I introduced them and put Valerie on the spot at once! Petronella, you see, asked her all sorts of things about Sydney that she couldn't possibly answer—and she jumped to the conclusion that she'd given herself away. So then she began to terrify the kid—told her not to talk about Australia again, or else——! It worked," said Georgie, "as Petronella's only nine."

"But what exactly *was* their plan?" asked Peter, when the indignation had died down. "Was Valerie a sort of vanguard?"

"Yes," Susan nodded, "that's exactly what she was. She had to spy out the land and make notes about the times the stables were unattended, and when the grooms have their free time, and so forth. Her mother was to come and take her out in about a fortnight's time, and Valerie was to make her report then. She had to pretend she couldn't ride."

"Of course she's jolly good really," said Georgie, "because they've always had a lot to do with horses. But she fooled us over that. Well, Sue's told you their plan—but Valerie didn't wait for her mother to come. She found out that Miss Primrose was going to buy some new ponies from a super stable near London, and rang up her mother to tell her. She wasn't allowed to use the phone, so she let two of the ponies loose after dark, and then shouted 'Help!' on the drive—just to get everyone in a tizzy. Then she rushed to the phone and told Ma Gaunt about Bramblemere . . ."

"My *dear!*" said Mrs. Kane. "A girl of sixteen?"

"Oh, she's more than that," said Susan decidedly. "Nineteen if she's a day. Mutton dressed as lamb!"

"They'd have seen through her all right at St. Monica's," stated Gerry. "You must be a trusting crowd . . ."

"On the contrary," said Mr. Kane, "they would have been very suspicious people if they *had* questioned this girl, thinking her Miss Primrose's cousin. What did you imagine had happened, Georgie, when Spot and the other horses were spirited away?"

"Why, Daddy, of course we all believed that Miss Primrose had engaged a new vet, and that he'd really called for them. I suppose we *were* a lot of mugginses," Georgie admitted, grinning at Gerry, who nodded in heartfelt agreement. "It was Valerie's father who collected them, you see, in a hired van. That was after they'd lured Miss Primrose to London."

"Yes, as soon as Ma heard about the Bramblemere stables she got her husband to ring up Miss Primrose, pretending to be the owner," gabbled Susan, "with some message about a setback to do with the new ponies she'd bought, which couldn't be put right till she came. Matron answered the phone when Miss Primrose was out riding, and gave her the message. It was meant, of course, to get her out of the way—and it worked. She went haring off to Bramblemere at once."

"If she'd only rung back the stables," Gerry remarked, with a sniff, "she'd have spoken to the real owner and found it was only a hoax."

"Another time," said Susan, glowering, "she'd better get in touch with *you*, and you can tell her what to do! Oh, sorry, Gerry. Go on, Georgie."

"All right, and I must be quick," said Georgie, "because I know the gong will go in a minute . . . The Gaunts had a huge piece of luck. They'd meant, you know, to meet Miss Primrose at the stables at Bramblemere, because Valerie managed to phone up and tell them she'd started. They were going to delay her somehow, long enough for Ma Gaunt to rush down to the Grange and arrange about selling all the horses and ponies she could lay her hands on. But it didn't work out quite like that. On the outskirts of London Miss Primrose had a crash. A lorry ran into her, damaged the car, and broke her right arm. She gave her nephew's address to the people who came to help her, and she was taken to his flat, while the car had to go into dock."

"Wait a moment—I'm getting out of my depth!" said Mr. Kane. "How was this lucky for the Gaunts? They must have been in a frenzy, wondering where Miss Primrose had got to!"

"Oh, they found out," Georgie explained. "They hung about, and when she didn't turn up, they asked at the stables, pretending they'd promised to meet her. And the owner told her that John Primrose had telephoned about the accident. So then they realized that they had to change their plans. Pa got his transport van into action, and Ma came down to take over the Grange. She soon made the stables 'out of bounds,' and kept us cooped up as much as possible, so that she and Valerie could get on with their job. They must have had their eye on all the pictures and valuables as well . . . Oh, it seems like a nightmare!" Georgie broke off to laugh. "And she was so mean that she even cut down our food and the hot-water supply! But it must have been pretty ghastly for them, wondering all the time when Miss Primrose was coming back."

"Why *didn't* she come back, or send her nephew, or at least let someone know where she was?" Tough asked bluntly.

"Because she had to find out first who the Gaunts were. Remember, she thought they were cousins. As soon as she found out that the real Bramblemere people had not rung her up at all, she told John the whole story, and he told their family lawyer. Investigations started—and it was agreed that Miss Primrose should lie low till they were finished. She knew the Kenpot would carry on," Georgie said. "Oh, the *time*—I must finish telling you! Miss Primrose came back at last—on the very day that the Kenpot had decided that *she* must go and tell the whole story to a lawyer, because of course the staff had realized by then that the Gaunts were phoney."

"The Kenpot was listening, apparently, when the

Gaunts tripped up over Waratah," chimed in Susan. "Valerie said it was like mimosa—she didn't even say wattle, as a real Australian would have done. And they knew they'd given themselves away—that's why Ma tried to stop us at the stables . . ."

"Booooom!" roared the luncheon gong at that moment, and there was a general move towards the house.

"But the horses, Georgie!" Mrs. Kane was quite pale. "You said in your letter that nearly all of them had been stolen at the last—except Withershins! What did those terrible people do with them?"

"Nothing really, thank goodness. They hadn't time. They turned them all into a paddock they'd managed to rent for the time being, about twenty miles away. Oh, it was lovely when they came home!" cried Georgie, smiling at Susan as they both relived that wonderful day.

"Well," said Gerry ponderously, "if the lawyer had worked it out, and Miss Primrose had come back all primed with the facts of the case, they didn't really need Georgie's pony clue, did they?"

"Didn't they?" flashed Susan, crimsoning with wrath. "They were pretty certain that Petronella was the real cousin, but they couldn't get in touch with the Parfitts in Australia, and so they hadn't proved how she was connected with the Primrose family. When they heard about the pictures of Sheltie in the cave, it gave them something to work on—and they soon found out everything they wanted to know."

"The Gaunts will be punished," Georgie said soberly, intent on telling her family the rest of the tale, "but I expect Miss Primrose'll see that they're let down as lightly as possible, because she's like that. The Thurstons say she's trying to get Valerie a job in Bramblemere stables, but I don't know. Anyway, now that everything's turned out so beautifully, we're going to forget all the rest."

As they stood aside demurely to let their visitors enter the refectory, which presented a gala appearance today, Georgie and Susan exchanged glances. One thing they would not forget was Ermyn, in her blue dress, walking downstairs that evening when all seemed lost, and how the sight of her had shown them what the old traditions really meant. Both realized now that they had gained far more than they had lost by that term's fantastic adventure.

Lunch was a very gay meal that day. Girls, mistresses, and visitors alike were light-hearted with relief to know that everything was back to normal now, and as for Petronella Primrose, she sat in her little kindergarten chair beaming impartially at everyone who glanced in her direction. She was happy now. She belonged.

It was a perfect afternoon, the sunshine growing stronger as, lunch over, the spectators began to wander up to Randall's Meadow, while the competitors flew up to their bedrooms to change. Through the open windows they could hear the thrilling chink of harness as Maxwell and the other grooms worked on the ponies.

The gymkhana began at half-past two, as daylight soon fails in March, even though spring *is* in the air. The field had been marked out that morning, and the local people who always acted as stewards on these occasions were there, and so was Mr. Evans, the vet, who had cast a professional eye at all the ponies and pronounced them none the worse.

Despite her injured arm, Miss Primrose took her rightful place at the head of things, and looked splendid, as usual, in her beautifully-cut riding clothes. A yell of delight went up as Mademoiselle, ridden by Miss Ruggles, won her jumping event without a single fault.

Georgie's family cheered wildly every time Georgie, Susan, or Ermyn went past on their respective ponies, and when Georgie and Spot most unexpectedly won the obstacle race, the whole assembly shouted its approval. "Darling Spot," Georgie whispered in his ear, and he turned to give her that special look that always made her wonder if he wanted to purr like King Toby, the wonderful golden cat at home, who was his great friend.

Penelope didn't compete, but she made a triumphal entry towards the end, led by Petronella, who was bursting with pride. And then Ermyn did some trick riding and won a partner race with Catherine.

"Oh, well done!" said a low voice just behind Georgie and Susan, who were watching this time; and they turned sharply, in utter amazement. For there was Constance, taller and thinner than they remembered, her eyes fixed on Catherine and Starbright.

"What luck—her arriving just in time to see that!" cried Susan, and then they had another surprise. Constance turned to them, laughing happily.

"Yes, wasn't it?" she said, as if she could hear just as well as anyone else. And then she told them. "I'm not really deaf any more! In a few weeks' time I'll be perfectly all right. It was that tumble, you know—I banged my head, and after a while I realized what was happening, but Mummy and Daddy thought we oughtn't to tell Cathy, just in case—— (There they are, by Miss Primrose; you must meet them presently). I'll tell Catherine now. Oh, Georgie! No more Morse!"

Georgie thought then how lovely it must be to hear, after a long silence, the happy sounds that were in the air today—the song of the birds, the wind in the trees which hid the Grange from this field, the laughter, the clamour of hooves, and the eager voices. "And next term we're having three Houses!" came suddenly from the small Petronella, who was chattering away, quite fearlessly, to the Conways' fierce Uncle Gordon. And, like a ripple, the words were repeated: "Next term—next term . . ."

"Grand Finale!" called one of the judges through the loudspeaker. "Keep behind the horse lines, *please!"*

Georgie edged Spot between Susan's Plum Pudding and Ermyn's Withershins. She imagined Ermyn's delight when she heard about Constance, but shook her head at Susan, who was longing to tell her now.

"After the Grand Finale, Sue!"

"All right," said Susan reluctantly, and then, as they had a few minutes' grace: "You know, the Kenpot makes mistakes like everyone else! She told us in English last week that, if a thing's perfect, it can't be *more* perfect. But"—she took a deep breath —"it jolly well can!"